NO NAME

Tim Tingle

7th Generation
Summertown, Tennessee

7th Generation, an imprint of
Book Publishing Company
PO Box 99, Summertown, TN 38483
888-260-8458
bookpubco.com
nativevoicesbooks.com

ISBN: 978-1-939053-06-0

19 18 17 16 15 14   1 2 3 4 5 6 7 8 9

Printed in the United States

Library of Congress Cataloging-in-Publication Data
Tingle, Tim.
 No Name / Tim Tingle.
   pages cm
 ISBN 978-1-939053-06-0 (pbk.) -- ISBN 978-1-939053-93-0 (e-book)
[1. Fathers and sons--Fiction. 2. Child abuse--Fiction. 3. Alcoholism--Fiction.
4. Friendship--Fiction. 5. Basketball--Fiction. 6. Choctaw Indians--Fiction. 7.
Cherokee Indians--Fiction. 8. Indians of North America--Oklahoma--Fiction. 9.
Oklahoma--Fiction.] I. Title.
 PZ7.T489No 2014
 [Fic]--dc23

Contents

Chapter 1: Under the Door and Before 1

Chapter 2: Orange Juice on the Floor 6

Chapter 3: Run! 13

Chapter 4: My New Digs 20

Chapter 5: Living in a Hole 27

Chapter 6: Backyard Submarine 33

Chapter 7: My Horror Movie 40

Chapter 8: The Boy with No Name 48

Chapter 9: How Bad Can It Get? 55

Chapter 10: Worse than You Think 59

Chapter 11: It Can Hurt to Listen 68

Chapter 12: Finally, Basketball! 77

Chapter 13: Clean, Hard Play 84

Chapter 14: Peace Offering or Trap? 94

Chapter 15: Johnny's Dad 103

Chapter 16: Mystery Lady Faye 113

Chapter 17: Crying over Spilled Juice 121

Chapter 18: My Turn to Be Dad 130

Chapter 19: Got It Bad, My Man 137

Chapter 20: Baptism by Car 145

Chapter 21: Is This a Dream? 153

About the Author 159

To my family of survivors: Mom Margaret; Dad Archie; the Tingle boys, Danny, Ricky, and Bruce; and most especially to my big sister, Bobbie Jeanne

Chapter 1
Under the Door and Before

Friday night, June 8

I am living under a door in my backyard.

I dug a deep hole behind a fat-trunked tree and dragged a junkyard door over the hole. I glued leaves and grass to one side, so no one can see it's a door.

There are no hinges. If anyone raked the leaves in the backyard (my chore for the past ten years), they would discover the door. The metal fingers of the rake would scrape scratches in the blue paint of the door.

And I would get in big trouble.

But I'm not worried. That will never happen. If anyone tried to rake the leaves, my father would grab the rake from them.

"Oh no, no you don't!" he'd holler, and the red veins of his neck would swell. "That's exactly what the boy wants! Somebody else doing his chores."

That would bother him more than my being gone for a week. But don't feel sorry for me. "That's exactly what he wants!" my dad would yell. And yes, the red veins of his neck would swell.

So I am living under a door to get away from my dad—Buck Byington, as his friends know him. I know nobody is looking for me. My dad has not reported me as a missing person to the police.

I heard him talking to his buddy Guy about me yesterday. Dad was sitting on the back porch and yelling into his phone.

"Mind your own business, Guy. I'm not telling anybody Bobby's missing. That's what he wants, for the cops and everybody in town to be looking for him. Somebody will call his mother and she'll get all upset and fly home. She's on vacation, Guy! She needs time away from that little punk."

Hoke. That's enough about where I am now. You need to know how I got here. (And before we get started, you should know that *hoke* means "okay" in the Choctaw language. I'm Choctaw, and I use *hoke* a lot. Hoke?)

Here goes:

Saturday morning, May 12, 2014 (almost a month ago)

"You need a ride to the airport?" Dad asked.

My mother was taking her first vacation from work in years. She had stayed up late last night washing clothes and packing. Dad went to bed early, after the ten o'clock news.

Something was happening, something more than a vacation. I'm sixteen years old and I'm not stupid. I'd learned a long time ago to pay very close attention to anything Mom and Dad said. "You need a ride?" Dad asked again.

Mom was carrying her heavy suitcase to the door. She put it down and stared at his back. He didn't even turn around. Finally, she hung her head and said, "No. Margie is giving me a ride."

"Umm," Dad said. When he didn't care either way, that's all he said. "Umm."

I dragged her suitcase out the door while Mom stood by the cottonwood tree that shaded the front porch. Margie was a friend of hers from work. In less than ten minutes, she pulled her red Buick into the driveway and Mom waved at her.

"Will you load my things in the car?" Mom asked me, then she stepped back in the house. I watched her lean over the sofa and kiss my dad.

"Umm," he said. That was his good-bye to her.

We loaded her bags into the trunk while Margie stayed in the car. Mom closed the trunk and stood with her back to me for the longest time.

I waited. When Mom turned to me, she had tears in her eyes. I wrapped my arms around myself. I hated to look at grown-ups crying, especially my mom.

"You be very careful, Bobby," she said.

"I will," I told her. "When are you coming home?"

"As soon as I can. I will miss you most of all. Do you know that?"

"I'll miss you, too," I said.

She kissed me on the cheek. "I'll call you at home early Saturday mornings," she said. "Before your father gets up."

"Hoke," I said. That was the last thing I said to my mom. "Hoke." Maybe that was better than "Umm." I hope so.

Margie backed out of the driveway. I stood in the yard and waved at Mom. When she was gone, I got my basketball from the garage. Dribbling all the way, I walked two blocks to the basketball court at the park.

I dribbled with my left hand, just like Kevin Durant. He was right-handed, like me, but he could go right or left, either way. He was impossible to guard.

Someday I'll shoot three-pointers like Durant, I said to myself.

Chapter 2
Orange Juice on the Floor

It barely rained all summer, so the leaves were already falling. I broke a branch from a scraggly oak and swept the basketball court clean. I hated dribbling a dusty basketball. Nobody was at the park, just some kids playing on the merry-go-round.

I always started with free throws. I dribbled twice, stared hard at the rim, and shot the ball. "Always follow through!" I heard Coach Scott holler in my mind. He was my gym coach in junior high.

I made six out of ten free throws. I was better than that. But I missed Mom.

So what happens now? I kept asking myself. *Who'll do the shopping? Who cooks supper? Who washes the clothes?*

"You lazy little punk! Who do you think will wash your dirty clothes?" That voice was also in my mind. It was my dad, yelling at me.

I stayed all day at the park. My friends from school showed up and we played half-court games—make it, take it. Whoever made ten baskets first was the winner. I was a good shooter from the corner and my team usually won. If somebody came out to guard me, I dribbled around him to the basket.

"High five," Johnny said after every basket, and we slapped palms. Johnny Mackey was a Cherokee and he was my best friend. He was also a great basketball player. He was tall and skinny, and when I missed a shot, he was always there to rebound and put it back in.

By early afternoon we were tired and sweaty.

"You want to come over for some sandwiches?" I asked Johnny. I'd been to his house a few times, but he'd never been to mine. We were friends from school.

"Sure," Johnny said. "You live close?"

"Two blocks thataway," I said, pointing to my street.

We dribbled and passed the ball back and forth on the way home. When we reached my house, I rolled the ball in the garage and closed the door.

"Let's go around back," I said.

Less chance of seeing Dad that way, I thought. But no luck. We stepped through the back door and Dad was sitting at the kitchen table.

"You think you're getting out of work now that your mother is gone?" he said. He took a long drink and slammed his can to the table. "I'm talking to you, boy!"

"I can work now," I said. "I went down to the park. This is my friend, Johnny."

"I know who he is," said Dad. "I know his old man. He thinks he's better than we are."

Johnny nodded to me and backed out the door. No sandwiches today.

"We are Choctaw, boy!" Dad yelled, loud enough for Johnny to hear.

I was ashamed about my dad, but I knew Johnny would be hoke. We were teammates. Nobody could dribble and shoot like me, and nobody could play defense and rebound like Johnny. Besides, everybody knew how my dad was. He always hollered when he drank.

And that made-up fight between Cherokees and Choctaws, that was for grown-ups to worry about. We had better things to do than fight old wars.

"I'll rake the leaves," I said, stepping out the back door.

"We got weeds in the flower beds taller than the house!" Dad said.

I didn't say anything, but I knew what I'd be doing till dark. No lunch today. I got me a drink from the water faucet and went to work.

Dad must have been "running on empty," as he liked to say. In an hour I heard him drive to the corner store, the mufflers on his pickup popping like shotguns.

I ran to the kitchen and made me a bologna sandwich, with mayo and dill pickles. My Choctaw family had a thing about dill pickles. They were hoke, as my grandma used to say.

I leaned against the house and ate my sandwich. I had a spot where the gardenias grew thick and Dad couldn't see me. I know, my dad wasn't even around.

But what if a Cherokee warrior shot out his tires with a bow and arrow and Dad came home to get a Choctaw cannon and blow every Cherokee off the map?

Hoke, that's not gonna happen. But you can't be too careful. Not with my dad.

I raked leaves in the backyard till well after dark. I pulled weeds till my fingers blistered and a bunch of fire ants crawled all over me. They were smart fire ants. They all stung me at the same time.

Legs, back, neck, ears.

"Yow!" I screamed. Dad was home now, watching TV and sipping his brew.

"If you ain't been bit by a rattlesnake, then shut up!" he hollered. I waited for the funny part of the joke. "And if it is a rattlesnake, you're dead anyway. So shut up till the undertaker comes."

I pulled my shirt off and brushed the ants away. I hung my pants over a bush and ran to the water faucet. I hosed myself down good.

"You hungry for some supper?" Dad asked through the open window.

"Yes, that'd be great."

"Good," he said. "I'm hungry, too. I bought a big can of chili and some cheese and onions. Your turn to cook."

I dashed through the kitchen, carrying my pants. Ten minutes later, dried off and decent, I cooked supper for us both. I sat at the table and ate while Dad watched TV. He fell asleep on the sofa that night. That was never a good thing. He always woke up mad.

The next morning I was sitting at the table, drinking orange juice and eating a bowl of crunchy chocolate cereal. He snuck up behind me.

"You know why I stayed up so late, you little punk?" he said.

I just looked at him. I had learned not to talk to Dad in the mornings. But this morning, the first morning without my mom, it didn't matter.

"You know why I stayed up late?" he asked me again. He gave me a mean look and walked away from the table. I thought I was safe, but I was wrong.

I lifted my orange juice glass and took a drink. At that moment, Dad grabbed the back of my chair and flung it to the floor. I hit my head hard. The glass shattered and orange juice flew all over the kitchen.

Chapter 3
Run!

I rolled to my feet and headed for the door, but the floor was slick. My legs flew out from under me. I fell face-first and my wrist landed on a sharp piece of glass. Blood flowed from my arm, making a wet puddle of blood and orange juice.

Dad grabbed me by the collar and lifted me. He drew back his arm to hit me, but he stepped in the puddle. He stumbled and waved his arms before he lost it. Dad fell backward and landed on the floor. He made a horrible face and the breath left him in a loud *whoof*!

Dad sat up slowly. He reached over his left shoulder and pulled out a piece of glass as big as a dollar bill. Blood gushed from the cut.

He looked at his hand holding the glass while the blood flowed down his arm. Then he tilted his head like he didn't know what was happening. I couldn't believe what I was seeing.

"Are you hoke?" I heard myself asking. He might be the biggest bully in town, but he was still my dad.

The look he gave me was unlike anything I had ever seen. It was like he realized, for the first time, what it meant to be my dad.

But that lasted only for a moment. Soon everything was back to normal.

Dad shook his fist at me. He called out, "I will get you for this, you worthless piece of dung!"

I ran from the kitchen, slamming the door behind me. Dad was mad now, really mad. My only hope was to run fast and far away. Not to the park. He'd look for me there.

Not to Johnny's. Dad was so mad he might come banging on Johnny's front door. But this wasn't the first time Dad really lost it. This wasn't the first time the veins in his neck swelled bright red.

I knew where to go.

The railroad tracks. They snaked through the woods a half mile away. There was no road to the tracks, not even a dirt road. And if Dad was crazy enough to drive his truck across the grassy field, he didn't know where the sinkholes were.

I could get away. Maybe.

I cut through backyards and hopped over a fence. Tall pine trees waved in the breeze. The woods looked friendly, and I needed friends—even if they were only trees. I hunched over and ran through the tall grass.

I was almost to the woods when it happened.

I had no warning. The grass grew so tall I never saw the hole. My foot sunk in the mud and I fell. My ankle twisted and I felt a painful "pop."

I landed on my back. My head hit the soft grass and I lay there, looking at the clouds floating overhead. I had been running scared for half an hour and I was breathing hard. My dad had thrown my chair to the floor and my world would never be the same.

Blood still oozed down my arm from the cut on my wrist. My ankle throbbed like somebody was pounding my foot with a rock. I crossed my legs so my ankle hung over my knee, but that only made it hurt worse.

Johnny had sprained his ankle once, so I knew what to expect. Several weeks of limping and wincing with every step. Not good. No running, no getting away.

"Now you're gonna get the whippin' you deserve!" I could hear my dad say. How many times had I heard this before?

"The whippin' I deserved" was always the worst kind. And it had nothing to do with what I had done. It had more to do with how much my dad had to drink.

I lifted myself just enough to look across the field. *Dad can't see me now*, I thought. *I'm safe for a while at least.*

I slid back into the hole and laughed, not a happy laugh but a sad, stupid little laugh—

the laugh you do when you feel really sorry for yourself.

"Yeah," I said out loud. "I'm real safe. I'm in the bottom of a sinkhole by the railroad tracks. My arm is cut and bleeding. My ankle is sprained, maybe broken. My mom is gone for nobody knows how long. I have maybe seventy-five cents in my pocket. My dad just pulled a piece of glass from his shoulder. He blames me for it, and he wants to give me 'the whipping I deserve.'"

There's no way out of this. That was my first thought. But I have spent my whole life figuring out ways to get out, get away, get anywhere else but where I was.

I'd also learned that sometimes the answer is right in front of you. This was one of those times. I was lying in a hole and nobody could see me. If I waited till dark, I could crawl out and get something to eat. My ankle maybe wouldn't hurt so bad.

If somebody walked by, they might see me. So I needed to cover up the hole. But what if Mom comes back? What if a snake slides down the sinkhole?

Hoke. So a hole was a good idea, a hole where Dad couldn't find me, but I needed a hole closer to home. I lifted myself again and looked to the houses. I couldn't see mine, of course, but I pictured our house in my mind.

The grass was overgrown in our backyard. That was my next chore. The leaves needed raking. I laughed for real this time. I had a plan, a crazy plan, but one that would work! I laughed so loud and long that I stomped my feet.

Yowwww!

My ankle didn't think it was funny.

Neither did I, but I was happy anyway.

I eased myself back into the hole and waited. I knew my Dad. After washing the cut on his shoulder, he would take a quick shower and drive to the Choctaw Clinic, where everybody knew him. He'd fuss and complain about me to everybody. And they would pretend to agree with him.

I was right. In less than an hour I heard the crazy-loud mufflers of my dad's pick-up truck. He backed out of the driveway and took off to town. I crawled out of the sinkhole and limped as fast as I could to the backyard. I knew I had at least a few hours before Dad returned.

Where to start?

Chapter 4
My New Digs

"Hoke," my music teacher always said, "begin at the beginning." I wanted a room of my own, where nobody could wake me up and drag me out of bed. I wanted a place to sleep and a place to hang out, maybe with a few friends. I wanted a place to chill out and do nothing if that's what I wanted to do. Nothing.

Hoke, let's get real. I was tired of being afraid, and I wanted a place away from my dad. I didn't want to spend all day worrying when he might hit me again. Now I couldn't even eat breakfast without worrying. He might flip my chair over and send me crashing to the floor.

I picked out a spot under the oldest tree in our yard, a red oak tree with a thick trunk. It was covered with leaves and surrounded by tall grass. Between the oak tree and the fence was the perfect spot. The tree trunk would block my dad's view.

I limped to the garage and found a shovel and a trash can. The dirt was soft and easy to dig. For the next hour I worked without stopping. I dug the hole and tossed the dirt in the trash can. When it was half full, I lifted it over the fence and dragged it to the sinkhole. It was more work than I thought, but I couldn't leave any sign of my digging.

After two hours and eight trips to fill the sinkhole with dirt from the backyard, I plopped to the ground, exhausted. My ankle was swollen bigger than a softball and throbbed like a powwow drum. But I was determined.

Dad might be home soon, I thought. *I've got to cover up the hole.*

I was sitting on the edge of the sinkhole. I lifted my neck high and looked from one side of the field to the other.

The junkyard! As every young Choctaw knows, if you look hard enough, you'll find treasures in the junkyard. Car parts, tools, broken toys that only need a wheel, all sorts of treasures. So limp, limp, limp, away I go!

At the very moment I gazed down at the junkyard below, the sun peeped through the clouds. A single ray of yellow sunshine shone upon my treasure, the answer to all the problems of my life.

Hoke, maybe that's a little overboard, but I did find what I was seeking.

I limp-dashed down the hill and scooted under the fence. Rusty old cars with broken windshields and no engines surrounded me. I climbed over a pile of sliced-up tires till I stood over the door.

The hinges were broken but I didn't care. The door was beautiful, pale blue as the morning sky. Where the doorknob used to be was a hole the size of my fist. The door was solid, with no cracks, no rotten wood or termites. It was the perfect roof for my new home!

The tricky part was getting the door from the junkyard to my backyard. If my ankle wasn't sprained I could do it. But every step I took was like walking on nails.

That's when I heard his voice again, almost like he was standing over me.

"Stop your whining, boy! We all got troubles. At least you got two legs to walk on. So stop whining and do it!"

I sat down and smiled. My ankle throbbed, but I had to smile. He was the meanest man I had ever met, but no matter how hard I tried, I couldn't get away. He was my dad and I was stuck with him. Now I was taking his advice.

I shook my head and laughed. I stood up, limped to the door, and tried lifting it. Not gonna happen, not even with a good ankle.

"Sorry, Dad," I said out loud. "I'm needing some help."

I saw him standing in front of me. Hoke. I almost saw him. It seemed like I saw him. He had his arms folded and he shook his head. He tightened his mouth and spit on the ground, like he always did when he was disgusted with me.

But when he lifted his eyes to look at me, I saw something new.

NO! I don't want to see this! This was not happening.

Dad, my dad, had a look in his eyes, one I never saw. And his face changed, too. Hoke. This sounds crazy, even to me. But Dad almost looked like he was proud of me, proud that his son was trying to lift a heavy door with a bum ankle.

"You are dreaming," I told myself. "You can't trust him. You know that."

I looked over my shoulder to my house. It was maybe half a mile away. Hoke. Time for some math. A half mile away was around eight hundred yards. I knew that from watching my cousin run track.

If I dragged the door a hundred yards a day, it would take me eight days to get it to the backyard. Too long. But two hundred yards a day—four days—that could work. That would give me plenty of time to dig the hole. And if Johnny helped me, if he dragged the door two hundred yards a day, I could have the door by late tomorrow!

"You lazy little punk! Stop whining and get to work!"

So I did. I dragged the door maybe ten yards and plopped to the ground. I lifted my pant leg to get a look at my ankle. It was purple. I could see swirls of blood veins, all purple and blue.

I need a new way of walking, I thought. I stood up and put my bum foot on the ground flat, without moving my ankle up or down. I used that leg like a cane. I put almost no weight on it. Then I stepped big and strong on my other leg. I let it take all the weight.

This was a funny way of walking, but it worked.

By sundown I had dragged the door all the way to my back fence. I thought about asking Johnny for help, several times. But when I considered how far it was to his house and that maybe he wasn't home anyway, it just seemed easier to do it myself.

"If you want something done right, you gotta do it yourself!"

"Will somebody make please make him shut up?" I heard myself asking.

Chapter 5
Living in a Hole

I dragged the door through the back gate and sat down, leaning against the tree trunk. In two seconds I was asleep. But not for long. I don't know what woke me up, but I jumped to my feet. I thought I heard Dad's truck coming down the street.

No, I must have been dreaming. But he would soon be home and I had work to do. I couldn't leave the door where it was. He could see it from anywhere in the house.

I hurried to the garage and found a big tube of powerful wood glue. I raked leaves and yanked weeds from around the house, where nobody would notice. They were my "camouflage," a word I'd learned from my Vietnam-vet uncle, Danny.

I glued the weeds and leaves to the door. I dug dirt from behind the fence and scattered it over the glue till the door was covered.

"When you do the right thing, you sometimes get lucky." Nope, not words from my dad. My mom always said this. My mom. I was so worried and working so hard to get away from Dad, I almost forgot that Mom was gone. Then I heard it.

Vrooom! Vrooom!

Dad's mufflers. Like a drop of blood falling from the ceiling in a vampire movie, Dad's mufflers meant everything was about to change. I saw the beams of his headlights against the back fence. I felt like a prisoner climbing over the prison wall when the searchlight catches him. I froze, just like the prisoner always does.

But I wasn't a prisoner. I had worked through pain all day so I could be free of him. I pulled the door to the edge of the hole and jumped inside, then slowly lifted the door over myself and the hole.

I wished I could climb outside, just for a minute, to see if the door looked natural, covered in dead leaves and weeds. But that wasn't possible. I was in the hole and Dad was in the kitchen by now. Even when he wasn't hungry or thirsty, he always went to the kitchen first.

It didn't take me long to see that this hole, my new home, needed some improvements. For one thing, I couldn't see or hear anything. Just me in the dark, dirty hole. This was not only boring but maybe dangerous.

What if?—I always made crazy stuff up by asking "what if?"

Hoke.

What if Dad sold the house and the new owners discovered oil in the backyard? What if I was sound asleep when they start the drilling? What if the giant oil drill pierced my stomach, and when it rose from the ground, my bloody body was dangling from it?

And what if my dad was watching, still mad that he never thought of drilling for oil in the backyard? What if he saw my bloody body hanging from the drill blade? I can hear him yelling at me.

"I don't care if I sold the house. Stop bleeding on the patio furniture!"

Hoke. Too much thinking. My hands went to my stomach. No bleeding, no oil drill. But I still lay in a hole. Soon it would be dark enough for me to climb out. Very quietly, in case Dad was sitting on the patio.

In a short while I climbed out and hid behind the tree. Dad was at the kitchen table, eating fries and a burger. He was wearing a T-shirt and bandages were wrapped all around his shoulder. As I watched, Dad closed his eyes and his head hit the table, scattering French fries all over the floor.

He must be taking painkillers, I thought. I remembered the look on his face when he pulled the glass from his shoulder.

I slipped through the back gate and limped to the park. The lights stayed on till ten o'clock every night. Johnny and some of his friends were hanging out, shooting jumpers and lay-ups. Nothing serious.

"Hey, man," Johnny said. Though I tried to hide it, Johnny saw me limping. "What's up?"

"Nothing. What's up with you?" I replied, ignoring his real question.

"We've been playing ball," Johnny said, bouncing the basketball and taking a long shot. "We're about ready to head home."

"Yeah," one of his Cherokee buddies said, "it's getting late."

They started leaving the park, but Johnny gave me a look that said, *Stay around. We should talk.*

"I'll see you guys tomorrow," he said. Once they were gone, he dribbled to the free-throw line. We didn't say anything for a long while. He shot ten free throws and I rebounded for him. Then I shot my ten. He made five; I made nine.

"You can still shoot, even with a bum ankle," Johnny said, shaking his head.

He stepped to the line and started on his second ten.

"How's things with your dad?" he asked. He was hinting for me to tell him what happened.

"Same old, same old," I said.

"He's sure got a temper."

"Yeah. And now that my mom is gone, it's worse than ever."

"What are you gonna do? I couldn't live with my old man if he was like that."

"I'm not living with him," I said.

"Where are you living?"

"In a hole in the ground. I'm living in a hole in the ground."

"Yeah," Johnny laughed. He dribbled a few times and shot another free throw. "I know what you mean. I'm living in that same hole!"

I waited a minute before I replied. I wasn't sure I wanted anybody to know.

"No, Johnny," I finally said. "I really am living in a hole."

Chapter 6
Backyard Submarine

"His pickup's gone," I said as we neared my house. "My dad's not here."

"We don't have to go through the house, do we?" Johnny asked.

"No way we're going through the house. I just wanted to see if his truck was in the driveway. Let's go around back."

Soon we stood staring at the door, the roof of my new home.

"So that's it, huh?" he asked. "How did you drag the door from the junkyard, with your bum ankle?"

"Wasn't easy. But it was that or living with the old man."

"Easy choice," Johnny said. "Uh, how long have you been down there? You haven't spent the night yet, have you?"

"Not yet."

"I got a question."

"Fire away."

"Where's the air hole?"

"The air hole?"

"Yes, the air hole. How do you breathe?"

"I breathe through my nose. Like anybody else. Why are you asking me that?"

"Because, my one true basketball friend, I do not want you to die of suffocation. With the door closed, you're gonna run out of air. I'm guessing in a few hours. Good thing you didn't spend the night down there."

"Johnny!" I said. "What kind of an idiot do you think I am? I thought of that."

Johnny laughed so loud I was afraid Dad would hear him, wherever he was.

"You don't lie that well," he said, still laughing.

I had to laugh, too. "Hoke, hoke, my one true basketball friend. So maybe you saved my life. What's the big deal?"

"The big deal is this. We better dig you an air hole."

We didn't say anything for a while. Johnny flipped the ball to me in an around-the-back pass. "Any ideas?" he finally asked.

"I'm thinking we should dig the air hole close to the tree. And we need some kinda pipe, so the ground doesn't cave in while I'm asleep."

"We can glue leaves over the end, so nobody can see it," Johnny said. "We've got some old plastic pipe in my garage. How long do you think it should be?"

I stretched my arms three feet apart. "How about this?"

"I'll be back in half an hour," Johnny said. "Keep everything under control while I'm gone. If your dad comes, hit him with a full-court press."

"Will do," I said. "And Johnny . . ."

"What?"

"Yakoke, big time." (You guessed it. *Yakoke* means "thank you" in Choctaw.)

"You're welcome. Big time, too."

While Johnny was gone, I sat behind the tree. A bright summer moon shone through the leaves. My ankle was throbbing and singing that old pain song, but I was used to it by now.

I pulled up my jeans. The purple streaks had turned black. I wiggled my ankle back and forth, real slow. It was stiff and sore, but getting better. I leaned against the fence.

"I'm lucky to have a friend like Johnny," I whispered to myself. Almost in reply, a robin flew from the tree, rustling the leaves above me.

That's when I had my first hint that I was not alone.

I glanced to the tree limbs and caught a quick motion from the house next door. Somebody yanked the curtains closed. Somebody was watching me from their upstairs window.

I was kidding myself. I knew who that somebody was. Carolina Faye. That's what they called her at school. She was a grade behind me, so I didn't know her that well.

What's she doing looking at me? I thought. It felt funny not knowing how long she'd been watching Johnny and me. *Maybe she's been watching me the whole time. Maybe she watched me dig the hole.*

I knew she wouldn't tell anybody. She didn't have any friends. She didn't play basketball or volleyball or run girls track. She didn't play the clarinet or twirl the baton. I tried talking to her once or twice, but she acted like she didn't hear me.

Faye and her mom and dad came from the mountains in Carolina. She was thin, but not too thin. She had shiny brown hair and she wore it long. She was a little shorter than me. Maybe she had nice eyes, but I never saw them. She always hid her face whenever I came around.

Now three people knew about my new home—Johnny, me, and Carolina Faye. For some strange reason, this didn't bother me, not one bit. Carolina Faye wouldn't tell anybody, and now I had an excuse to talk to her next time we met.

When Johnny returned, he carried a plastic pipe.

"It's the biggest pipe I could find," he said. "You should be able to move it around like a telescope and see everything in the backyard."

Johnny was right. He stuck the pipe through the ground and poked a branch in it to clean out the dirt.

"Give it a try," Johnny said.

He lifted the door and I eased myself into the hole. Looking through the pipe, I could see the patio and the back of the house.

"I bet I can hear Dad's truck," I said. Johnny was standing above the hole. He heard every word I said.

"You gotta remember," Johnny said, "if he's sitting on the patio, he can hear you too."

"You have a flashlight I can borrow?" I asked him. "It's dark down here."

"I thought you'd never ask," he said. "Careful. Here it comes."

He pulled a flashlight from his back pocket and put it in the pipe. The flashlight twisted and rattled down the pipe, landing in my lap.

"Thanks," I told him.

"No prob," he said.

I turned on the light and saw my new world for the first time. The dirt wall was dark brown and covered with tiny white roots. Somehow it seemed alive. I shined the flashlight beam from one wall to the other.

I wanted my rug, the rug from my bedroom. I wanted a picture on the wall, a picture of Johnny and me playing basketball. We didn't need anybody else.

After Johnny left, I climbed out of my room. Dad was staying gone a long time. *I hope he doesn't drive on those painkillers,* I thought.

I looked to the moon and had the strangest feeling. I wished my dad was home. I was worrying about my dad. That had never happened before.

Chapter 7
My Horror Movie

Hoke. So he swerved his truck when he turned into the driveway. Hoke. So he smashed the plastic trash can. Hoke. So what if it was the neighbor's trash can? Hoke, already!

I knew Dad would blame me for everything that happened. He always did.

"I never drank before you came into my life!" That's what he'd yell at me. I heard him tell Mom the same thing a few weeks before she left.

But he was home and I was glad. That night, when I climbed into my underground room, I could fall asleep knowing he was safe.

Earlier, before he came home, I'd spent the evening running stuff from my bedroom to my new home. I hung my picture of the

Oklahoma City Thunder on a thick root sticking through the ground. I had enough snacks to last me through breakfast. And I could sleep on the blue-and-white Indian rug from Santa Fe.

I fell asleep peacefully, with no nightmares. Then, just after midnight, it happened, like in the horror movies. Maybe my life is a horror movie.

"I'm gonna kill him! Just wait till I find him. I'll whip him so hard he won't sit down for a year!" Hearing my dad holler—and not knowing it was a dream—I jumped up and got ready to run.

Pow! (That's the sound of my head bumping on the bottom of the door. It hurts way more in real life, trust me.)

"Ooooow," I said, muffling my voice with my hand. I didn't feel any blood, but I knew I'd have a fat purple knot by morning.

"If he thinks he can stay out all night, he's got another think coming!"

Who is he talking to? I wondered. I looked through the pipe. Just like in the horror movies, the moon was covered in clouds and I could see only shadows. Dad was sitting on the patio. At first I thought he was yelling into his cell phone.

Then the wind blew the clouds from the moon and I caught a glimpse of his favorite drinking buddy, Mr. Robison. He was a history teacher at the high school, but he worked with my dad at the lumberyard for the summer.

"Thanks for coming over," my dad said. Dad liked Mr. Robison, I figured out, because he only drank a can or two. He was always sober enough to drive.

"Never too late for a nightcap," Mr. Robison replied. "Besides, somebody had to clear your neighbor's trash can out of the driveway. I tossed it in your garage so they'll think somebody stole it." He laughed at his own dumb joke.

I could hear everything they were saying through the pipe. This was weird. I didn't like it. I knew my dad hated me, but I didn't like hearing him talk about me to somebody else.

"If that kid hadn't run away, I'd never have smashed the trash can," Dad said.

That's crazy, I thought. *He smashed the trash can 'cause he was drunk.*

But here's the strange thing. Mr. Robison didn't say anything. My dad thought he agreed with him, but I saw something else. Mr. Robison rolled his eyes back, like you do when you hear something ridiculous. He didn't correct my dad, but he didn't agree with him.

Maybe there's hope, I thought. *Maybe not all grown-ups are crazy.*

Seeing the world from my hole in the ground was really strange at first. But I learned something very important that evening. If you watch people, really watch them, especially when they don't think you're watching them, you see them better. You get to know them better.

I saw a Mr. Robison my dad didn't know. Mr. Robison didn't blame me for the trash can. He didn't blame me for my mom leaving. He blamed my dad for everything that was happening.

I could see it in the way he looked at my dad.

I grew more and more sleepy. I pulled the lookout tube under the leaves and fell asleep. When I woke up, the lights were out in the house. I needed to stretch my legs. I lifted the door and crawled from the hole.

My ankle was still sore, but not as bad as yesterday. I made sure the lights were out all over the house.

No need to drag the door over the hole, I thought. *I'll do that when I return.*

I walked through the back gate and into the field. The clouds still floated across the moon like in those horror movies. I stood and stared at it for the longest time. But this was no movie. This was real.

I didn't know how real till I climbed into the hole an hour later.

I settled against the dirt wall and curled up, ready to sleep. I pulled the door over myself and wrapped the blanket around me. I thought I heard something move. I shined my flashlight on the opposite wall.

A face stared back at me, a strange, inhuman face. The head of the thing sat on a short, chubby body, like a dwarf. Large paws swatted the air, and it came for me.

"Turn that thing off! You're blinding me," it yelled.

I flipped off the flashlight. "Mr. Robison?" I said. "Is that you?"

"Yes, it's me," he said. "And you need to be a little more careful, son. Didn't your momma ever tell you to look before you climb in a hole in your backyard?"

"No," I said. "She never did."

I was still scared, even though I knew the movie monster was really my dad's friend. "Why are you here?" I asked him.

"I could ask you the same thing," he said.

"How did you know I was here?"

"Son, your dad doesn't pay much attention, to you or anybody else. I saw that pipe sticking up from the ground. I helped your dad to bed and thought I'd do some exploring. Sure enough, I found this hole."

"How did you know it was mine?"

Mr. Robison tilted his head and gave me a funny look. "Hmmm," he said. "This is the backyard of your house. Your dad says you're not around anymore. There's a rug and picture from your room." He laughed a friendly laugh and gripped my shoulder.

"Son, you're not a bad kid. Maybe you'll come through this mess all right."

I wasn't sleepy anymore. I was wide awake.

"Are you going to tell Dad?"

"No, not yet. I'll tell you what. I won't tell your old man. When you are ready, you tell him."

"I'm too scared to tell him. He'd whip me worse than ever. You don't know what he's like when he gets mad."

"Oh, yes I do," Mr. Robison said. "You're not the only one he gets mad at, trust me."

"I'm the only one he whips when he's mad."

Mr. Robison didn't reply. He gave me a look that said, *You're too young to know the truth.*

Kids my age see that look a lot.

"You'll know more when you get older," he said. "If you have time to listen, I have a story for you."

I had to laugh at that. "If I have time to listen," I said, laughing as I spoke. "If I have time to listen! Mr. Robison, you sneak into my secret house under the ground and ask me if I have time to listen? Where would I go?"

Mr. Robison laughed too. Maybe this was the first time in my life I ever shared a joke with a grown-up. He wasn't like my mom, always nervous. Or my dad, always mean. Mr. Robison was hoke.

"Is it a short story?" I asked. "I have to sleep soon. Busy day tomorrow, you know."

"Yeah, busy day hiding from your dad. No, it's not short, but I'll grab your foot if you start to fall asleep."

"Great," I said. "Hoke, let's hear it."

Chapter 8
The Boy with No Name

"First off, Bobby, you have to understand," Mr. Robison said, "this is an old Choctaw story, one I heard from my uncle. I'm gonna remember it as best I can."

I nodded and he continued.

Hoke, a long time ago there lived this Choctaw boy with no name. In those days you had to earn your name by being really good at something, like maybe stickball or hunting or fishing. And the elders would give you a name.

But No Name, and that's what they called him, he wasn't that good at anything. He was just an average kid. And his dad didn't like that, not one bit. Every morning he'd wake

him up, hollering, "No Name! No
Name! How can I ever be proud of
a son with no name?" That's what
he'd say, every morning.

I knew where this was going and I didn't like
it. This was gonna be a story about me and my
dad. I dug this hole to get away from Dad, not
to hear stories about him. But I knew better
than to interrupt a grown-up, so I just shut up
and listened.

And every morning No Name would
run to a tree in the backyard and
cry. But he wasn't by himself. A
girl called Whispering Wind lived
nearby. She moved as soft as the
wind and barely even rattled the
leaves when she walked.
   And this is what she did. Every
morning she crept up behind him,
wet her lips, and kissed him, right
behind the ear. "Yowwww!" he
would holler.

"Do you know what happened then?" Mr. Robison asked me.

I shrugged my shoulders and wrapped my arms around my knees. Of course I didn't know what happened next. Mr. Robison was one funny dude.

Whispering Wind stood there with a sweet little smile on her face. And every morning she said the same thing: "No Name, No Name. I will always love you, even though you have no name."

But No Name was so mad. He rubbed his wet ear and shouted, "I don't love you! Leave me alone!"

Then he grew to be ten years old, and nothing changed. Every morning his father would shake him and wake him. "No Name, No Name, get up! Go hunting, go fishing! Play stickball, do something! I can never be proud of a son with no name!"

And every morning Whispering Wind snuck up behind him. Every morning she wet her lips with her tongue and kissed him, right on the ear. And every morning he ran to the woods yelling, "Leave me alone!"

Then he grew to be twelve years old. In the old days, when you turned twelve years old, you became an adult Choctaw. There was a special celebration day and families came from miles around.

After a day of food and visiting, the twelve-year-olds were lined up on the banks of the river. A Choctaw elder stepped into the water and everyone grew silent. This was like a baptism, but it was before Christianity came to the Choctaws, way before.

One by one the old man led the twelve-year-olds into the water. When the water was waist high, he put his arm around their shoulders and whispered in their ear. He whispered words for only them to hear, words for life.

As No Name stood waiting, he looked for his father. He couldn't see him anywhere. Everyone else in his family was there, his grandparents and cousins, but not his dad.

Soon the elder led No Name into the water. He wrapped his arm around his shoulders and whispered, "Be brave and go into it. You will know when. He needs you."

No Name closed his eyes, held his breath, and the old man dipped him into the shallow waters. When he lifted him from the river, No Name was a grown-up Choctaw. He stepped to the shore and an old woman met him with a blanket. She dried him off and he sat close to the campfire.

For hours the Choctaw elders told stories to the young ones, about other tribes, other nations that were our friends, and who our enemies were. They talked about the funny trickster Rabbit, and about giving to others—for that is the Choctaw way.

As the ceremony drew to a close, the Choctaw chief rose to speak and everyone grew silent. "This is the most important lesson of all," he said. "No matter how mean someone has been to you, you must always find a way to forgive them."

Mr. Robison didn't say anything for a long time. He just looked at me. I knew who he was talking about. There was no getting away from my dad.

"What if he beats you and tells you you're a piece of dung?" I asked.

"What if he loves you but doesn't know how to say it?" Mr. Robison replied.

"Shut up about my dad!" I shouted. "He doesn't love me! I don't want to hear this!"

I pulled my shirt over my head and cried. I didn't care if Mr. Robison heard me or not.

"You're no better than my dad!" I said. "Just go away. I never asked you here."

But he didn't go away. He waited for me to finish crying and hollering. I wiped my face with my shirt and looked up at him. Mr. Robison had the saddest look on his face.

"I'm sorry I made you cry," he said. Even in the darkness I could see shiny tears on his cheeks.

"I'm sorry, too," I said. "I didn't mean to yell at you."

"Do you want me to go?"

Of course I wanted him to go, but I couldn't say it. I just couldn't be that mean to him. So I lied. Even though it meant he'd be around for who knows how long, I lied.

"No, don't go," I said. "I want to hear the rest of the story." (Another lie!)

Chapter 9
How Bad Can It Get?

"Hoke," he said. "Where were we? Oh yeah."

After midnight the ceremony was over and people were tired. Some curled up in their blankets and slept by the fire. Others started walking home.

No Name's mother said to him, "Son, I am going to your aunt's campsite and taking your sister with me. You can walk home by yourself. You'll be safe."

No Name nodded and started walking, all by himself. "This is my special celebration day," he said to himself, "and I am alone, just like always."

But as he neared his house, he saw a fire in the fireplace. He wondered what was happening and looked through the window. His father was sitting by the fire! No Name smiled the biggest smile of his life.

He looked to the starry sky and spoke aloud. "This was the plan all along," he said. "My father was at the river, hiding in the shadows. He saw me go into the water. They wanted to surprise me. That's why my mother is staying with her sister, so my father and I can have this time, just the two of us! We can have our first man-to-man talk! This is the happiest day of my life."

No Name stepped into the house, scared and happy at the same time.

He had never really noticed how big his dad was. As he stood up, his father spread his arms. They cast huge shadows in front of the fire, shadows that wrapped around the whole room. No Name stood and stared, waiting for his father to speak.

And when he did, his voice was deep and strong. "No Name," his father said, reaching for him. "No Name, come to me, son. I am so proud of you."

But when his father said the word "proud," something happened. He grew angry, just like before. He put his hand on No Name's chest and closed his eyes. "No Name," he said, spitting on the floor. "No Name! How could I ever be proud of a son with no name?"

He shoved No Name so hard the boy stumbled backward, out the door and down the steps. He landed hard on his back and the breath left him. As he lay on the ground, No Name felt more grown up than ever. It wasn't the tears running down his cheeks that felt grown up.

It was the sobbing—deep in his chest—a sobbing that he knew would never go away. His father slammed the door and threw water on the fire. Smoke filled the house, and his father left through the back door.

Mr. Robison stopped talking. I was crying again, just like No Name. I wrapped my arms around myself and rocked back and forth.

"Make the hurting go away," I said. "Can you please make it all go away."

I came to my senses and waited for Mr. Robison to tell the rest of the story. But he couldn't, not yet. Mr. Robison was crying, too.

"You are Choctaw too, Mr. Robison. Aren't you?" I asked.

"Yes, Bobby, I am Choctaw."

"Was your dad like No Name's?"

"No. I had a good dad."

"You were lucky," I said.

"I know, Bobby. I miss him."

Chapter 10
Worse than You Think

We both sat for a while without saying anything. Finally I spoke.

"Mr. Robison?"

"What?"

"Can I ask you something?"

"Go ahead."

"Why are you telling me this? It won't do any good. My dad hates me and that's never gonna change."

"I agree with you about one thing, Bobby. Your dad is mean, as mean as anybody I've ever met. If he did in public the things he's done to you and your mother, he'd be in jail. For a long time."

"Then why are you his friend?"

"Sometimes I ask myself that, Bobby."

Neither of us said anything for a long time, but I knew he wanted to tell me something about my dad.

"I have seen another side to your dad," he finally said. "With your mother gone and now you out of his life, your dad has had to admit, probably for the first time ever, that *he* is the problem. He's brought all of this on himself."

"Did he tell you that?" I asked.

"Yes, he did, Bobby. When he's sober, he's a different man. But, hey, that's enough about your old man. Let's get back to the story, how about it?"

"Gladly," I said.

"Hoke," he said.

No Name finally stopped sobbing. He stood up and walked to the tree where Whispering Wind was waiting for him. Somehow he knew she would be there.

She touched his shoulder. "No Name," she said, "I will always love you, even though you have no name."

He hung his head before speaking. "At least somebody does," he said. "At least somebody does."

As he walked to the woods, she followed him. And for the first time, her feet crackled on the dry sycamore leaves. No Name could hear her. He took her by the hand and they walked to the river. They sat all night on the riverbank and watched the yellow moon sparkle on the water.

And then he grew to be sixteen. The age of sixteen is another important time, for at the age of sixteen a Choctaw boy can go to battle if war is declared.

The young boys were excited. "We can earn new and braver names," they said, and No Name whispered to himself, "And I can earn a name at all."

But the older Choctaws, they prayed for peace. They knew that war brings death and they wanted none of it. But in this story, the young people had their way. A group of Creeks came far too close to Choctaw town, and Choctaw scouts were sent out to see what the Creeks wanted.

When the scouts reported back to the Choctaw Council, they weren't worried. "They have no weapons," the scouts said. "They're only cutting firewood. Maybe there is no wood in Creek country."

The older council members were not convinced. "There is more wood in the mountains of Creek country than in these Choctaw swamps," they said. "Keep an eye on them."

But the young scouts didn't listen. They returned to the Creek camp and fell asleep on their watch. As soon as the Creeks saw them sleeping, they gathered bundles of wood. Very quietly, they snuck to the edge of town and stuffed the bundles under Choctaw houses. Then they set fire to the wood and dashed away.

Soon the houses caught fire and Choctaws ran from their homes. They passed baskets of water back and forth till the fires were put out.

But this was a horrible thing to do, to burn people's homes while they slept. The Choctaw Council met that night and war was declared on the Creeks. The young men of sixteen were excited. "We can show how brave we are," they said.

For four days the Choctaw men taught the young ones the ways of war. They taught them how to use new weapons and how to be so quiet not even the animals could hear them.

At noon of the fourth day, they built a fire. The young men circled

the fire and the old men chanted a
war song.

Way ho hanah hey yo
Halo hey ya hey hey yo
Way ho hanah hey yo
Halo hey ya hey hey yo

Way ho, hanah hey yo
Way ho hey ya hey hey yo!

The young men circled the fire,
slowly at first. Then faster and faster
they danced, till the spirit of the fire
leaped into their hearts and they
became warriors. They trailed after
the Creeks that very night. The trail
led by his tree, and No Name leaned
against it. He knew she would be
there. She kissed him softly and
said, "No Name, I will always love
you, even though you have no name.
You must be careful. Please come
back to me."

No Name spoke in the voice of a warrior, ready for battle. "I will bring back a brave name," he said. "You will see."

Whispering Wind cried as she watched him go. She knew he had not heard her message. The Creeks left an easy trail to follow. They walked on the path, where anyone could see their footprints. "They are stupid," the young men said. "See how easy it is to follow them!"

But the older warriors knew better. "They fooled the guards," they said. "They are leaving a trail for us to follow. It might be a trap."

After several days they entered Creek country, the state of Georgia today. The pine trees stretched to the sky. Soon they came to a cave on the side of a mountain, surrounded by boulders.

The footprints of the Creeks led inside the cave. "We have them trapped inside!" the young men said. "There is no way out. We have them now!"

But the old warriors shook their heads. "They are too smart for this," they said. But on this sad day for Choctaws, the young men won out. They convinced the older ones the Creeks were trapped inside. Soon every Choctaw warrior, old and young alike, lifted their spears and bows and charged into the cave.

They left only No Name outside, to guard the entrance. But there were no Creeks inside the cave. Instead, a hundred Creeks surrounded the cave, hiding in the boulders.

They knocked No Name out with a rock and pulled him aside. They dragged a wooden gate to the entrance of the cave, so no one could get out. The gate was made of green cypress wood, to burn smoky and slow.

They set fire to the gate and the flames shot up, making thick clouds of green smoke. They fanned the smoke into the cave. The Choctaws ran to the entrance, but they couldn't move the gate. They coughed and began to fall. And die.

Soon there was only one Choctaw still alive inside the cave. He kept his face to the ground where the smoke wouldn't settle.

Chapter 11
It Can Hurt to Listen

"Please stop!" I said to Mr. Robison. "I don't want to hear this. I don't want No Name to die. Did the Creeks kill him?"

"Bobby, you have to trust me. Sometimes we have to go through all sorts of bad times before anything good can happen."

"Will the good ever come?" I asked.

"Yes, good will come. And the bad times make you strong," he said.

"I'm tired of hearing that! Maybe I don't want to be strong. Maybe I just want to live like a normal kid."

"Maybe we all want normal lives, Bobby. But nobody has it easy."

"Hoke," I said. "I'll trust you. But No Name better live."

"The Creeks didn't kill No Name," Mr. Robison said. "They let him live to tell the story."

After they left, No Name woke up. He saw the burning gate. He knew his friends were trapped inside. He ran to the gate and tried to pull it down.

But the gate was heavy and his hands were burned. Then he heard the voice of the old man in the river, from when he was twelve. "Be brave and go into it," the old man said. "He needs you."

No Name walked to the gate. He grabbed the burning boards and climbed them like a ladder. When he reached the top, he rocked and rocked till the gate fell on top of him.

"You lied to me!" I shouted. "You said No Name lived!"

"I told you the Creeks didn't kill him," Mr. Robison said. "But trust me, Bobby, this is a good story."

"I might listen and I might not, but I am mad at you," I said. "Hoke, go on."

The Choctaw man who was still alive saw what No Name had done. He tried to pull the gate off of him, but it was too heavy. Ten minutes later, he kicked the burning embers aside.

No Name was wrinkled and breathing his last breath. But in the old days there were people who had the spirit touch, and this man had the touch. He put his fingertips on No Name's temple and lifted his face to the sky. "Holitopama," he said.

And his spirit left him. Whoosh!

And No Name entered his body. Whoosh!

It was a very strange thing, to be in the body of another. For several days No Name wandered in the woods, discovering who he was. The Choctaws came and found the bodies. They carried them back to Choctaw country.

But when she came, Whispering Wind, she grew angry. "I told him to be careful," she said. "I told him I would always love him, even though he had no name!"

When she returned home, she threw herself on her bed. She refused to eat or drink. When they brought her food, she flung the bowl against the wall. "I don't want to eat!" she said. "I don't want to live."

One day No Name entered the town, in the body of another. He went to her house and said to her mother, "I would like to see Whispering Wind." Her mother looked at him strangely. This young man had never called on her before, but he was the only one to return from the battle, so she stepped aside.

No Name knelt by her bed. "It is me, No Name," he said. "I have come back for you."

She opened her eyes with hope, but when she saw the face of another, she grew angry. "This is a trick," she shouted, "to bring me back to life. It will not work!" She put her palm on his chest and, with all her strength, shoved him out the door.

No Name stumbled backward and hit the ground hard. He asked himself, "How could she do this? This is what my father did. How could she do this to me?"

And then he smiled. "This is a sign," he said. "I know what to do."

No Name entered her room, so quietly she didn't know he was there. He leaned close to where she lay on the pillow, and he kissed her behind the ear.

She sat up and yelled, "What are you doing?"

No Name stood up and laughed. "I am doing what you did to me for all those years. And then you would say, 'No Name, No Name, I will always love you, even though you have no name.'"

Then he knelt beside her and took her hand. "I have come back for you," he said. "No one else could know this but me. Please, come back to me."

Whispering Wing closed her eyes, and when she opened them, there he was. No Name. And then it was the face of another—but she knew, somehow, that No Name had come back to her.

He lifted her and took her to the river to drink. On the way back they picked berries, and that night they cooked pashofa, Choctaw corn soup.

A week later, they were married, telling no one who he was.

And a month later came the time to end the grieving. Everyone in town gathered, with all the kinfolk. They told stories over a campfire, stories of the ones they had lost. Finally it came time for the last one to speak, the father of No Name.

Everyone grew nervous when he stood before the fire. "You are right to be nervous," he said. "Every day you have heard me yell at my son. I was so mean to him. But now, I feel so bad. I would give my life, this night, if I could spend a day with him and let him know how much I loved him. But now he is gone and I cannot."

Then came the time for the one who had returned to receive his new name. No Name, telling no one who he was, stepped before the fire. "I would like to choose my own name," he said, and the elders agreed.

No Name cast his eyes around the fire, looking at everyone, till finally he saw his true father. "I choose for myself a good name," he said. "I choose for myself a strong name. From this day forward you can call me No Name."

His father lifted his head and looked at his son, and somehow he knew. And this was a secret they kept until death. Every month, No Name and his father would go hunting or fishing together. Sometimes they went to the coast, sometimes to the woods. But wherever they went, they were together, father and son.

And No Name and Whispering Wind lived a long and happy life.

"Now," Mr. Robison said. "What do you think of the story?"

"Hoke," I said, "you're off the hook. But I still didn't want him to die."

Chapter 12
Finally, Basketball!

"Hoke," Mr. Robison said, "I better get home. My wife is already worrying."

He climbed out of my room and was about to leave—but he hesitated, like he remembered something important. He knelt down and leaned over the edge.

"I'm coaching the high school basketball team this year," he said.

"I thought you taught history."

"I do, but now I'm the basketball coach, too. Ever thought about playing high school basketball?"

"Dad would never let me. I have to sneak away to the park to play."

"Just leave your dad to me," Mr. Robison said. "You can have supper with my family after practice. I'll tell your dad he won't have to fix your supper."

"Are you kidding me?" I asked. "Dad never fixes me supper. I fix it for him."

Mr. Robison didn't say anything, but I knew what he was thinking.

"I'm beginning to understand why you dug this hole," he finally said. "But don't worry, son. I'll clear everything with your dad. You do want to play, don't you?"

"I'll play on one condition," I told him.

"What's that?"

"I'll play if Johnny plays," I said. "He's the best rebounder in town. And he plays good defense, too."

"Funny you'd say that," said Mr. Robison. "I was at Johnny's house earlier today. He said he'd play only if you did. He said you were the best three-point shooter in town. Sounds like we have the makings of a pretty good basketball team."

"Mr. Robison, Dad won't let me play."

"Want to bet?" Mr. Robison said. "If he says yes, you have to mow my yard next Saturday."

I had to laugh at that one. "Hoke, Mr. Robison. Either way, I win!"

"So do I," said Mr. Robison. "See you Saturday."

He pulled the door over my room and was gone. I leaned back and thought about everything that had just happened. *Mr. Robison knows where I am. But I trust him. He won't tell Dad. And what if I do get to play basketball? Wow! That would be so cool.*

In a few minutes I fell asleep. But not for long.

Knock! Knock! A loud knocking on the door woke me up.

"Mr. Robison," I said, "I thought you were gone."

"This is not Mr. Robison," a soft voice replied. It didn't sound like Mr. Robison. Not even close.

"Who are you?"

"Faye, from next door."

"Carolina Faye?"

"Yes. Can I come in?"

"Does anybody know you're here?"

"No. I know your underground room is a secret."

A secret, I thought. *Some secret. First Mr. Robison and now Carolina Faye knows about my secret room.* But I didn't want any more visitors, not this late.

"Faye," I said, "you need to go home. Dad might hear you."

"You dad is sound asleep," she said. "Don't you want some popcorn?"

"Popcorn? You brought me popcorn in the middle of the night?"

"Not exactly," she said. "I brought you a microwave oven."

"What? Are you crazy?" I asked her.

"That's not nice. But I'm not going away, not till you take the microwave."

I slid the door aside and Carolina Faye lowered herself into the hole. Then she turned and lifted a small microwave oven from the yard to my room.

"That's not gonna work down here," I said. "There's no electricity."

"I already thought of that," she said. "I bought the microwave and a long extension cord at Goodwill yesterday. I plugged the cord into a socket on my back patio. I already tried it and it works."

"Still not gonna work," I said. "My dad will see the cord."

"I'm a step ahead of you," Carolina Faye said. "I glued leaves all over it, like you did the door."

"I don't know what to say," I said, staring at the microwave.

"Try thank you," she said.

"Hoke, thank you."

Faye smiled and took a bag of ready-to-pop popcorn from her purse. "Now, let's cook some underground popcorn."

While we waited for the popcorn to pop, I didn't say anything. This adventure was speeding along too fast for my liking. First Mr. Robison appears. While I was glad about maybe playing basketball, I didn't like him knowing my secret. And now the strange girl next door shows up, very uninvited. I didn't like that one little bit.

Faye ripped open the bag and we started eating popcorn. It was buttery and good. I was about to ask her if she brought sodas, as a joke. But before I could say anything, she pulled two cans of grape soda from her purse.

"Here," she said, handing me one.

"Thank you." I took a long swallow before I spoke. "Faye, I know you are trying to help me. But this won't work."

"What do you mean?" she asked.

"You can't come over any time you want to. Somebody's gonna see you."

"I'll be careful," she said.

"No. Faye, listen to me. You don't know my dad. If he even suspects I'm hiding out here, I'll have to run away. Far away."

"I know your dad has a bad temper," she said. "I'll be careful."

"Faye, as long as I am down here, I can feel safe. But not if you are gonna come over whenever you want to."

Carolina Faye and I ate our popcorn and drank our sodas without saying another word. When we finished, she stuffed the empty cans and popcorn bag in her purse.

"I won't come over, ever again, unless you ask me," she said.

"Thank you. I don't mean to be rude," I said, "but I'm down here for a reason."

"I have something else for you," she said. She reached in her purse and pulled out a cell phone. "My big sister left this when she went to college. It still works."

"I can't take that," I said. "I don't have any money."

"It's a gift," she said. "Just don't get it wet. You know how to use it?"

"Yes. I can use a cell phone. I might live underground but I'm not an idiot."

Faye laughed really loud, then covered her mouth quickly.

"Oops. Sorry," she whispered.

I shrugged my shoulders. I didn't need words to tell her, "See what I mean!"

Chapter 13
Clean, Hard Play

Of course I was lying about knowing how to use a cell phone. After Faye left, I pushed a button and the phone came to life. I pushed the same button again and everything went dark.

"Hoke," I said to myself. "My first cell phone. Cool. An Indian with a cell phone. And I already know how to turn it on and off." I put the phone in my shirt pocket and fell asleep.

The next morning I woke up and the size of my problem slapped me in the face. I was on the high school basketball team, a really big deal. So was Johnny. I couldn't live in my underground room and go to school. And if I didn't go to school, I couldn't play basketball.

Hoke, now I'm beginning to understand, I thought. *Mr. Robison's no idiot. He thought of this all along. Oh well, school's still two months away. Something's bound to change.*

I looked through the pipe at the house. No sign of Dad. I lifted the door and crawled behind the tree. I leaned against it for a few minutes, listening. Still no Dad.

I scrambled over the fence and ran to the park, forgetting all about my ankle. I knew he would be there, getting ready for his first season on a real basketball team. Johnny waved a little wave at me, then turned and shot a free throw.

We were both so cool about this whole high school basketball thing. For two minutes. He made a free throw and tossed me the ball. I hit a three-pointer from the corner. Johnny gripped the ball with one hand and dribbled a few times.

Then he dropped the ball and looked at me. He ran to the basket, leaped up, grabbed the rim with both hands, and shouted, "We're on the team! Uniforms! Cheerleaders! Out-of-town games on the school bus! Practice every day after school! At the high school gym!"

I dribbled the ball and shot a long one. Johnny was still hanging on the rim.

"Not in my house, you don't!" he hollered, swatting the ball across the court and all the way to the kids' merry-go-round.

I jumped up and pounded the air with my fists. "Yeah!" I shouted. "We gonna win some ball games. Me and you, Cherokee Johnny, we gonna win us some ball games!"

We didn't see them, not at first. We didn't see the four Nahullo boys, wearing school jerseys, pick up the ball and amble our way. They were seniors and they'd played on the school basketball team since seventh grade.

"What team you think you gonna play on?" the tallest one asked. "We already got our team. You couldn't even warm the bench, not on our team."

Johnny and I just looked at each other.

"Wanna play some half-court?" Tallboy asked.

"Be hoke," Johnny said.

"Cool," said Tallboy. "Let's see. We got six players. So who wants to play with the redskins?"

The others shook their heads and laughed. "No way. I ain't playing with those losers," said one.

"Then I guess it's two on two," said Tallboy. "Make it, take it. Whoever scores gets to keep the ball. You want the ball first?"

"Sure," Johnny said.

Tallboy walked to him, as if to hand him the basketball. When he was only a few feet from Johnny, he flipped him a hard two-handed pass. The ball hit Johnny in the face.

"Gotta be ready if you want the ball," Tallboy said, and they laughed.

Johnny clenched his fists. I knew what he was thinking. He was trying to decide if he should bust Tallboy in the jaw or let him get away with it.

Part of me was hoping he'd smash the Nahullo punk in the face and bloody his nose. But another part of me knew what would happen. We were the Indian kids, the new kids. That would be the end of basketball for us.

"What's the matter? You got some chicken mixed in with that Cherokee blood?" Tallboy taunted.

That told us everything we needed to know. If he knew Johnny was Cherokee, Tallboy also knew we'd been asked to join the team. Word gets around fast in a small town.

Of course they knew. That's why they came to our neighborhood.

"I'm not afraid of you," Johnny said. "OK, so you caught me by surprise. Let's see what you can do with the ball. You take it first."

Johnny tossed him the basketball.

"Bart, let's take these punks," Tallboy said. A short, muscled-up boy nodded and slapped his palms together. The other two moved off the court and the game began.

Bart tossed the ball inbounds to Tallboy, who went to work right away. He backed into Johnny hard, almost pushing him to the ground. But Johnny kept his balance and pushed back.

Tallboy swung his elbow at Johnny, but Johnny was ready. He knew Tallboy would play dirty.

He dodged the elbow and went for the basketball. Before Tallboy knew what had happened, Johnny stole the basketball. He tossed it to me, and I sank a long shot from the corner.

"You lucky pile of buffalo dung!" shouted Tallboy.

"Yeah," Johnny said. "He's lucky. I never saw him do that before."

I stepped out of bounds and tossed the ball to Johnny. He had his back to Tallboy, so when the elbow came he didn't see it. Tallboy smacked him hard in the jaw and Johnny's lip burst open. Blood dripped on the leather basketball.

"Let's go, Johnny," I said. "We don't need this."

"Yeah, that's a good idea, punk," said Tallboy. "Go back to the rez where you belong!"

"Not just yet," Johnny said. He turned and faced Tallboy. Blood ran down his neck and covered his shirt. He didn't do anything to stop it, like he didn't notice. "I know you're strong. I know you can play dirty. But I want to know if you can play basketball."

Tallboy didn't reply. He looked at his buddies and laughed. "You hear that?" he said. "He's dumber than I thought."

His friends laughed too. "He don't know a tail-kicking from basketball," said Bart.

"We know the difference," Johnny said. "But I guess we are dumb about one thing. When you said you wanted to play basketball, we thought you were serious. We want to see if you guys are basketball players."

"You still wanna play us?" Tallboy asked.

"Yes, we do. And you got your punch in," Johnny said. "I give you that. You're the seniors. We're the punks. OK. But no more. Clean, hard play. Can we agree on that?" Johnny wiped the blood from his mouth and reached out his palm for a handshake.

Tallboy looked over his shoulder. His friends waited for him to decide. "All right with me," Tallboy said, slapping Johnny's hand.

The next hour was some of the toughest basketball I've ever played in my life. I did get elbowed in the ribs, more than once. And I gave it back.

Johnny was shoved to the court when Tallboy dove for the ball. But no more elbows to the mouth. No more laughing and name-calling. Tallboy was a good player, better than we thought. He had a smooth jump shot and could shoot a nice hook shot with either hand.

But he went for every fake. He was easy to drive against, easy to shoot over.

We split the first two games. "Next winner's the champ," Tallboy said. "And we get a substitution. Darrell, you ready to play?"

A quiet Nahullo boy stood up. "I'm always ready," he said. He walked on the court, rolling his arms around and lifting his knees to warm up. Johnny and I looked at each other. Darrell was Tallboy's secret weapon.

We took the ball first. I threw it to Johnny and he tossed it to me in the corner. Darrell was under the basket.

He's waiting for the rebound, I thought. *He's not even gonna guard me.* I took a dribble and got ready to shoot.

In the next two seconds everything changed.

Darrell wasn't waiting for the rebound. He was baiting me to shoot. I took my time, and when the ball left my hand, Darrell was ready. He took two long steps and jumped as high as the rim. He swatted the ball over my head and into the trees.

"Wow!" I said.

"Wow times two," Johnny said.

"Nice block," Tallboy said. "By the way, my name is Jimmy. And me and Darrell are starters on the team." He had a big grin on his face, a friendly grin.

Johnny and I played as hard as we could, but Jimmy and Darrell were good. Darrell was too tall for me to guard. He leaped over me and banked the ball off the backboard for the game winner.

"Nice game," he said, and shook my hand.

"Yeah, good game," Jimmy said. "It's time for us to hit the road." As they crossed the park to their car, Jimmy walked behind the others. We turned to shoot a few more baskets before heading for home, so we didn't see Jimmy return.

"How's your mouth?" he asked Johnny. "You gonna be OK?"

"No problem," Johnny said.

Jimmy touched his fist to his chest and nodded. Though no words of apology were said, this was Jimmy's way of saying "I'm sorry."

Johnny nodded back. I was proud of him, proud of us. Jimmy and his friends circled the park, honked and waved, and sped away. Johnny and I were now official members of the high school basketball team.

And why? Because Johnny was smart enough not to fight.

Chapter 14
Peace Offering or Trap?

"How did you do that?" I asked Johnny. We were getting close to my house and I saw Dad's truck wasn't in the driveway.

"Do what?" Johnny asked.

"Stay cool when he busted you."

"I learned that from my uncle," Johnny said.

"I never saw a Cherokee take it from a Nahullo," I said.

Johnny laughed. "Hey, not all Cherokees are hotheads. You've been listening to your dad too much. Besides, my uncle's not Cherokee. He's a white dude, married to my aunt. I used to spend summers with him, before we moved here. He's a lawyer in Durant. At least he's living there now."

"That's the Choctaw capitol, Durant," I said.

"Yeah, my uncle's working for the Choctaw Nation."

"Doing what?'

"Some fight over who owns the water rights. He says the state of Oklahoma is trying to drain Choctaw lakes."

"Yeah, I heard the chief talk about that last Labor Day. Those lakes are in Choctaw Nation, Johnny," I said, remembering Chief Pyle's speech.

"Hey, bro, I'm with you," Johnny said. "Big time."

"But what does that have to do with taking a dirty punch?" I asked him.

"Well," Johnny said, "my lawyer uncle says if you pay attention, you can see who's gonna win a fight before it ever starts. I looked around the basketball court this morning. I saw four of them and two of us. They outweighed us by maybe forty pounds apiece. And they are athletes. We didn't stand a chance."

"Unless we could keep it on the court," I said. "Smart move, Johnny."

"Thanks. Now, what's up with your old man?"

"Nothing changes," I said. "He's mad at me and happy with his beer."

"Something's gotta change," Johnny said. "You can't live underground and play basketball. You have to go to school. Make good grades."

"Hey, Johnny! You my friend or not?" I shouted. "I don't want to talk about it!"

Johnny didn't say a word for a long time. We walked around the house and climbed over the fence. "How long before Mr. Robison tells him where you are?" he finally asked.

"I'm hoping he won't tell him. Ever. He knows what my dad will do to me. He remembers the time I missed school for a few days. Dad got mad and kicked me. Cracked two ribs."

"What did your mom do?"

"She lied for him," I said. "She told the principal I fell off the roof. But she's tired of lying for him. That's why she's gone."

Johnny stopped and stared down at the door. I could tell that he didn't want to crawl underground with me.

"Dad's not home," I said. "Let's sit on the patio."

"Sure thing," he said.

"If he does come home, we can hear those mufflers from a mile away."

Johnny nodded and we sat down on the patio. He took the same folding chair Mr. Robison had sat in the night before. I sat where my dad always sat. I felt a little funny doing that. I was thinking maybe he could tell I'd been there.

"Hey, what's this?" Johnny asked. He lifted a sack from under the table.

"I don't know. What's in it?"

"Looks like a sandwich, potato chips, and a bottle of lemonade. And there's a note on the sack."

"What's it say?" I asked.

He read it to himself and put the sack on the table.

"You better read it," he said. The look on his face was strange.

"Hoke," I said, reading out loud. "If you ever come home, this food is for you, Bobby. Your Dad."

Sometimes, no matter how bad things are, they are what they are. You know who likes you. You know who doesn't. You wake up in the morning and know the world you live in.

But this was one of those times when everything changed. I hated it. I hated him. I could not be in my hole anymore. I had to tell somebody.

"I hate him!" I yelled. "I hate his guts!"

"He left you a sandwich, Bobby," Johnny said. "Maybe—"

"Shut up! I hate you, too. You and Mr. Robison and anybody who thinks things can change. Just shut up! I don't want my old man's food. I want him gone. I want him dead!"

Johnny lifted his head slowly. He looked at me like he had never seen me before in his life. He shook his head.

"You don't want that," he said. He closed his eyes and hung his head. He felt bad for me, I could see it. He knew I had said something I would regret for the rest of my life.

He was right. I didn't want my dad to be dead and gone. I wanted him to care for me. I wanted him to care for my mother. But the first time he tried to show he cared, by leaving me a sack of food, what did I do? I yelled and screamed and said I wanted him dead.

I stood up. I picked up the sack. I lifted it over my head, to fling it over the fence for the rats and ants to eat. But I didn't fling it over the fence.

"Yakoke, Johnny. You're a good friend," I said. I sat down and tore open the bag of chips. I split the peanut butter sandwich in half and handed him the lemonade.

"We can share the lemonade," he said. I nodded. We didn't say anything for five minutes. We chewed the sticky sandwich. The peanut butter had melted and was running all over the table. We chewed the chips and traded swigs of lemonade.

We never looked at each other. Then Johnny started laughing.

What does he have to laugh about? I thought, staring down at the table. But that was strange—to be having a meal with your friend and not even be looking at him.

I glanced up and saw Johnny licking peanut butter off his lips and laughing. I couldn't think of anything to say.

But I felt a stupid grin creep across my face. Soon I was laughing too. My Cherokee buddy Johnny and I laughed till our bellies were sore.

I took a drink, but I couldn't keep it down. I spit lemonade all over the table. Johnny took a long drink of lemonade and spit it all over me!

"Hey!" I shouted. "That's not funny!" But of course it was. It was even funnier when I took a handful of potato chips and dashed around the table. I tossed Johnny's Cherokee cap to the yard and crushed the chips in Johnny's hair.

We rolled on the ground, wrestling and laughing. After a while we lay back on the grass and tried to catch our breath.

"This laughing takes a lot of energy," Johnny said.

"Yeah. Why are we laughing anyway?"

"I don't know," he said. "Maybe laughing is better than crying."

"Yeah. I guess so," I said. "I have plenty to cry about."

"You have plenty to be thankful for, too," Johnny said. "When's the last time your dad made lunch for you?"

"Been a while."

"And we're on the basketball team, Bobby!"

"Wow," I said. "That's hard to believe."

That's when we heard Dad's truck. The mufflers rattled and roared. He was turning into the driveway.

"Hey man, I better be going," Johnny said.

"Yeah. Me, too. Going to my hole. See you later, Johnny."

Johnny climbed over the fence and I ran to the door. I slid it aside and jumped inside. I waited just long enough to give Dad time to park his truck. *He'll come to the patio to see if I ate lunch,* I thought.

I looked through the pipe and what I saw made me cry out loud.

"No!" I covered my mouth and hoped he hadn't heard me. I started to push the door open and run for it. But there was no time.

Johnny's Cherokee baseball cap was lying a few feet from the table.

Chapter 15
Johnny's Dad

Please, don't let him come outside, I prayed.

But I knew he would. He opened the back door and smiled. He saw the sack was empty and the food was gone.

Then he did something I never saw him do. He put his hands together and bowed his head and closed his eyes, like he was praying.

"You ate your lunch, son," he said. "Thank you, Lord, for bringing him home."

I wished the sun would set and the day would end, with my dad thanking the Lord for me, his son. But the day was not over, not yet.

My dad saw it. Johnny's baseball cap.

"Oh no," I whispered.

Dad picked up Johnny's cap. Even from twenty feet away, looking through the plastic pipe, I saw his face change. I saw the red veins in his neck swell. His chest moved back and forth and I knew he was breathing hard.

The dad I didn't know, this thankful-for-his-son dad was gone.

I closed my eyes and put my hands over my face. I couldn't help myself. I knew he would hit me hard. *What am I doing?* I thought. *He can't get me here.*

But even in my secret room, Dad was never far away. He threw Johnny's cap against the side of the house. He balled up his fist and looked ready to slam it against the brick wall. Then he remembered. The last time he did that, he broke two fingers. He had to drink his beer with his left hand for a month.

Dad shook his fist and looked to the sky.

He's taking back everything he said, I thought.

Dad kicked the folding chair where Johnny had been sitting only a few minutes ago. The chair flew through the air and landed on top of my room.

"No, please no," I said. I was afraid Dad would cross the yard and pick up the chair. He couldn't see my room, but if he stepped on the door I was in big, big trouble. He would rip open the door and I would be a trapped fox in the shotgun of my father's fists.

But he didn't come for the chair. Instead, he grabbed Johnny's cap and stormed through the house, slamming the door hard behind himself. I heard the mufflers roar.

"He's going to Johnny's house," I said. "He's going to my best friend's house and there is nothing I can do." I gave my dad a few minutes, to make sure he was gone. Then I climbed out of my room and dragged the door over the hole.

No time to waste, I thought. I hopped over the fence and started running. I took the shortcut to Johnny's house, across the field. As I ran, I felt my cell phone in my shirt pocket, bouncing against my chest.

"Yes!" I shouted. I sat down and made my first-ever cell-phone call, on my new phone!

"Hello," Johnny said.

"Bad news, Johnny," I said. "My dad just found your cap on the patio."

"Uh-oh."

"Yeah. Uh-oh is right," I said. "He just pulled out of the driveway. He's coming after you, Johnny. He thinks you found the food and ate it yourself. Are your folks there?"

"My mom's gone shopping, but Dad is here. What should I do?" Johnny asked.

"Explain to your dad what happened. My dad will be there any minute."

"I better warn my dad," Johnny said. "I gotta go. Trust me, Bobby, it'll be okay. See you later."

Johnny hung up the phone and I just stood there staring at the phone. There was nothing I could do. I looked across the field. My eyes stopped on the hole where I had sprained my ankle.

That seemed like years ago. I remembered dragging the door and digging the hole.

"I am not helpless," I said. I ran as fast as I could to Johnny's yard. I slipped through the gate and hid behind some rosebushes in his backyard. Through a window I saw Johnny and his dad sitting at a table. Johnny was talking and his dad was nodding and listening. Johnny was waving his arms and talking fast.

Suddenly Johnny stopped talking. His arms froze in midair. His dad looked to the front of the house. They heard the mufflers before I did.

My dad was pulling into their driveway. Johnny's dad stood up and left the room. Johnny stayed where he was, waiting for the storm. I ran across the yard and knocked on the window.

"Johnny," I whispered.

When Johnny saw me, his eyes grew big and he waved his hands in front of his face. "No," he said with his lips. Over and over he shook his head. "No!"

I hurried to the rosebushes and knelt close to the ground. Through the window I saw my dad and Mr. Mackey talking.

Hoke, they were not really talking. When my dad was mad, nobody talked. Dad yelled.

The veins on his neck swelled and everybody else listened.

I have maybe seen my dad this mad once or twice in my life. And now he was standing in the house of a Cherokee man. And if that wasn't bad enough, this Cherokee man made more money than Dad. He drove a nicer car. He lived in a big two-story house, with two new cars in the garage.

Even with the door closed and me hiding in the backyard, I could hear him holler. "You people move in and you think you own the town!"

I tried hard, but I couldn't stop myself from crying. "Dad, what is wrong with you?" I whispered.

All of a sudden Dad pulled back his fist, ready to throw a punch. Mr. Mackey didn't move. For a long moment the two men stared at each other. I was too scared to breathe. Then my dad flung the back door open and walked to the patio. He still held his clenched fists in front of him, ready to fight.

"You might own the town," he yelled, "but you don't own my house. Your kid came onto my property and ate my son's lunch. Somebody's gonna get a whipping. You or your son, who's it gonna be?"

Johnny's father walked slowly out the back door. He wasn't hollering. He didn't even seem mad. He acted like he and my dad were having a normal conversation.

"Mr. Byington," he said. "You are mad, I understand. I'd be mad, too. My son will pay for what he did."

"I want to see you give him the whipping he deserves," Dad said in a mean whisper. "With my belt!"

He leaned close to Mr. Mackey's face. His cheeks were blood red and he looked like a crazy man. Dad unbuckled his thick leather belt and whipped it into a loop.

"I don't need your belt," said Mr. Mackey. "I have my own."

"I'm not leaving till I see him whipped."

"Johnny!" his dad shouted.

"Yes, sir," Johnny said, stepping to the patio.

"Is this man telling the truth? Did you go into his backyard without his permission and eat his son's lunch?"

"Yes, Dad," said Johnny.

"Bring me the whipping cane," Mr. Mackey said. Johnny entered the house. In less than a minute he appeared, carrying a dark wooden cane. "After your whipping, you will go to your room. Do you understand me?"

"Yes, sir," Johnny said.

"Mr. Byington, I need privacy, please. I promise you, his punishment will match the crime."

"Give him one for me," Dad said.

Mr. Mackey nodded, but kept his eyes on Johnny. Soon Dad's mufflers screamed loud enough for everyone in the neighborhood to hear.

I didn't want to see Johnny get whipped with a cane. But I couldn't leave, not now.

"Lean over the table, son," his dad said. "Now, think of what you did. You are about to get the whipping you deserve, do you understand?"

"I think I do, Dad," Johnny said over his shoulder. "You're not gonna change your mind, are you?"

Johnny's dad laughed. "No, son. Here," he said, "take your whipping."

He tapped Johnny a few times on the backside with the cane. "Here's one for being dumb enough to leave your cap on that man's patio," Mr. Mackey said. "I hope you've learned your lesson."

"Are you finished?" Johnny asked.

"Yes, son. How did I do?"

"You did fine, Dad," Johnny said. "But do I have to go to my room?"

"That was the promise. I'll go get us some burgers. That be okay?"

"Sure, Dad. Thanks."

"Oh, just a minute," Mr. Mackey said, turning to face the rosebushes. "Bobby, you like French fries or onion rings with your burger?"

I stood up, feeling pretty foolish. "French fries will be fine," I said. "Thank you."

"Great. And you're welcome to visit Johnny if you like."

I felt like a five-year-old kid. I hung my head and walked by Mr. Mackey without looking at him. I wasn't sure what I had just seen, but I knew one thing.

Johnny's dad was nothing like mine. Johnny and his dad—they liked each other. This was different from anything I'd ever seen. A dad liking his *son*? A son liking his *dad*? What was this about?

Chapter 16
Mystery Lady Faye

When my granddad—my mother's father—
was still alive, he used to like those old black-
and-white movies. In the films, it was always
foggy at night and nobody could be trusted.
Everybody had a secret. My next-door
neighbor Faye watched everything from her
upstairs window. She would have fit perfectly
in an old movie. She knew everybody's secret.

At least she knew mine. When the phone
rang, I knew it was her.

"Your dad knows," she said.

"My dad knows what?"

"He knows enough," she said. "Just be
careful. He left you another sandwich on
the patio. But he's watching to see if you
come for it."

"How do you know?"

"Never mind about that," she said. "You have been warned."

Before I could say another word, Faye hung up. She didn't say good-bye, she just hung up, like a mystery lady in one of Granddad's old movies. But she was right. I had been warned. By Mystery Lady Faye.

I snuck around to the back and climbed over the fence—behind the tree, so he couldn't see me. I slid the door aside and climbed into my room. When I looked through the pipe, I saw she was right. Another sack sat on the picnic table.

This was too much for one day. First my stinking-mean old dad made me lunch. And when he thought somebody else ate it, he was ready to kick some rear end. Not just because it was Cherokee Johnny, but because he thought Johnny had taken my lunch. My dad was protecting me.

And now?

He made another lunch for me.

Hoke, I thought. *Let's see how much he's really changed.* I couldn't believe what I was doing. I climbed out of my room. I hopped the fence, walked around to the driveway, and entered the backyard through the gate. Like a normal person.

I spotted the sandwich, the sandwich that was supposed to be a surprise. So I tilted my head, like I was wondering "what's that?" Next thing I knew, I was sitting down and eating my peanut butter sandwich. The phone rang. I knew it was Faye, so I didn't answer. I knew what she would say.

The next thing that happened scared the pants off me. A voice came from behind me—a deep, dark voice like Darth Vader's.

"You like the sandwich?"

"Uh-huh," I said, nodding and chewing while I said it. I didn't dare look up.

"I been missing you, son."

Now I didn't know what to say. I took a giant bite of sandwich and chewed like my life depended on it. I was shaking inside.

"Oh, I forgot your soda," he said. In less than a minute he plopped a glass filled with ice-cold root beer in front of me.

"Thank you," I said, still chewing.

"Maybe this time the glass won't end up in my shoulder," Dad said, laughing. But this laugh was a soft one, more like Mr. Robison's. Not mean like my dad's.

But this *was* my dad, and when I looked up at him, he nodded at me. "Mr. Robison says you gonna be on the basketball team this year," he said.

"If you let me," I said. I was so scared. Can you understand why? My dad might get mad at anything. He might bang my head against the table and start cussing. I never knew, and neither did my mother.

But something was different this time. My dad and I were talking, almost like Johnny's dad talked to him.

"Of course, son. I already told Mr. Robison it was hoke."

"That means I have to mow his yard for free next Saturday," I said. Even I had to laugh at this. And what did my stinking-mean old dad do? He put his hand on my shoulder.

"I'm proud of you, Bobby."

I almost dropped my root beer glass. Mr. Robison's story washed over me like a flood. The word "proud," that was what did it. I waited for Dad to get angry and start hollering, "I could never be proud of a son with no name!"

But he didn't holler. Instead, he asked me, "Where you been staying?"

I could have said anything. I could have told him any lie and he'd never know the difference. But I knew it was now or never. If I wanted to play basketball on the high school team, I had to go to school, and I had to make the grades. And I could not do either from my hole-in-the-ground room.

If Dad hit me or beat me or cracked my ribs or slugged me in the face, then I would just have to leave home—run away or something, I didn't know. But then I couldn't play basketball, and I wanted that more than anything.

So I took the risk. I decided to give my dad a chance.

"You promise you won't get mad if I tell you?" I asked him.

"Is it that bad?" he said.

"No, Dad, just kinda crazy. See, I never really left home."

"What are you talking about?" he said. "You've been gone for a week."

"You wanna see where I've been staying?"

"You've been hiding out in the garage?" he asked.

"No, Dad, you're too smart for that. You would have caught me easy."

"Then where?"

"Follow me," I said. I stood up and walked across the backyard. Dad followed. When he stepped around the tree, he still couldn't see the door. The leaves and branches did their job.

"You've been hiding in a tree?" he asked, looking at the tree limbs above us. "How could you sleep up there without falling?"

"Come over here, Dad," I said, leading him to the door. "Stomp the ground here."

He had a funny look on his face, like I was playing a joke on him. But he stomped, and when he did, the wooden door shook.

"What's happening?" he asked. "What did you do?"

I didn't say anything. I pulled the door aside and held my palm out, pointing to my room. "Did you dig this?" Dad asked me.

"I did. All by myself. I didn't want to leave and I didn't want to stay. I didn't know what else to do," I told him.

"I know the feeling," Dad said. "Mind if I join you?"

The next thing I knew, I was sitting in my underground room with my dad. I pulled the door over us.

"Want some popcorn?" I asked.

"You got popcorn?"

"I can have." I pulled my blanket off the microwave.

"You know that won't work without electricity," Dad said.

I tossed a bag of unpopped popcorn in the microwave and shut the door.

"Push the button, Dad." He looked at me, still thinking this had to be a joke. When he pushed the button and the microwave lit up and whirred, he jumped so high he bumped his head on the door.

"Wow!" he said, ignoring the head bump. "Hoke, son, you got some explaining to do. I'm not mad, I promise. But tell me what I've been missing for the last week."

For the last week? I thought.

Chapter 17
Crying over Spilled Juice

So I told him. I told him how afraid I was after he cut his shoulder. I told him everything, even about Mr. Robison. My dad hung his head and listened the whole time. When I was finished, he reached across the room and shook my hand.

"Thank you, son. Yakoke," he said. "Thank you for trusting me. Now, I want to trust you with some stuff even your momma doesn't know about. But first, why don't you get us some cold drinks from the house? Here, I'll hold the door for you."

For the next hour, my dad and I ate popcorn and sipped cold drinks, sodas for me and beer for Dad. I heard about his life growing up. I knew he had eight brothers and sisters. I'd met some of my aunts and uncles once or twice, but they all moved away and we never saw them anymore.

"You wanna know why my family never gets together?" Dad asked.

"Because you live so far apart," I said.

"Yeah," he nodded, "but there's another reason. It's *my* dad. I know I'm not easy to live with. He wasn't either. He started drinking when he got home from work every day. He drank all weekend. Every Saturday he had his first beer right after breakfast. And he was a mean drunk. My dad beat us all—my mom, all eight of his kids."

The whole time he was talking, I was remembering the times my dad had kicked me and hit me for no real reason. I wrapped my arms around my knees and hid my face. He stopped talking and I knew he was looking at me, reading my unhappy thoughts about *him*.

Without looking up, I finally asked him, "He's gone now. Why don't you all get together now?"

"Son, when you've lived that way for so long, the last thing you want to do is bring back the memories. If we saw each other, we'd be right back in that old miserable life, the life we ran away from."

"You don't have to talk about it, Dad, not if you don't want to," I said.

"Hey, Bobby," Dad said. "I haven't told you the good part!" He was smiling in that strange new way.

"Hoke, Dad," I said. I took a long sip of root beer and got ready for the good news.

"When I was your age, I wanted to play basketball. All my brothers were football stars, local heroes. I was skinny as a kid, but I was quick. The outdoor court was only a block away, and me and a friend used to practice any time I could get away. We dribbled, we practiced long set shots, lay-ups, and jump shots once we were strong enough. And we were good, 'cause nobody in our part of town cared about basketball. It was all football— all year long.

"So when I told my dad I wanted to play basketball, he put his hand right here." Dad pointed to his chest and I heard his voice change, almost like he was about to cry.

"Right here," Dad continued. "He shoved me so hard I hit my head against the coffee table. I still have the scar." He moved his hair aside and showed me a two-inch scar over his forehead.

I didn't know what to say or do. I just waited for a long time, and when he didn't say anything, I did something so crazy I still can't believe I did it.

I lifted my shirt and leaned to the side, so Dad could get a good look at the scar from my cracked ribs.

When Dad spoke, he was stuttering and doing his best to hold back the tears. "I have hurt you, Bobby, just like my dad did me. I have, haven't I?"

I nodded.

Dad shook his head, and when he reached out for me with his powerful arms, I flinched. I covered my face with my hands and backed away.

"No, Bobby," he said. "I don't want to hurt you, ever again." Dad gripped me by the shoulders and pulled me to him. He held me for the longest time.

"Hoke," he finally said. "This was supposed to be the good news. Well, the good news is this. My dad never saw me play a game. He fussed and cussed and did everything he could to stop me from playing. But since he was drunk all the time, I never missed a practice."

Good news? I thought. *He can't forget the bad times.* So I did something I had never done before. I reached over and touched my dad on the knee.

"Good news?" I whispered.

He looked at me and smiled.

"You're right, Bobby," he said. "Here's the good news. When Coach Robison told me you were gonna be on the team, my whole world cracked apart. I told him, 'My son can't play basketball!' Then he said something I'll never forget. 'There's a lot about your son you don't know, Buck.'"

"That's what he told me. Everything cracked and the memories came flooding out. How bad I wanted my dad to be proud of me, but he never was. Never. But I can make it different for you, son. I want to help you be the best basketball player you can be. I am already proud of you. Coach Robison says you're the best three-point shooter he's ever seen."

The next thing that happened only happens in movies.

But this was no movie. This was more real than any moment of my sixteen years of living. We both started crying. No, we both started sobbing. We shook and sobbed, and then we hugged each other. That's what I said. Me and my dad *hugged* each other.

"So you've been playing my favorite sport in the world and I had no idea," he finally said.

I nodded and wiped my eyes dry.

"My Bobby," Dad said. "A basketball player." He shook his head and laughed.

We sat still for a long time after that. "I'm getting kinda stiff," Dad finally said, rubbing his knees. "Getting to be an old man myself, I guess. I'm heading to the house. You're welcome to come home if you like."

"Is it hoke if I stay here again tonight, Dad?"

"Sure. Just be up around sunrise. I'll have breakfast ready, served on the patio." I couldn't believe he said that. He lifted the door, climbed out, and turned around to say good-bye.

"See you in the morning, son. Sleep well." And he was gone.

But my night wasn't over yet.

Ten minutes after Dad was gone I heard a knocking on the door above me.

"Dad?" I asked.

"No, I am not your dad," Faye replied. "How about pulling the door aside so I can join you?"

Hoke. This night was getting to be a little weird. Hoke, more than a little. It had to be after midnight, and I was not used to visitors at this hour. But it was Faye, Mystery Lady Faye.

I lifted the door and she squeezed between the crack.

"What's up with you?" I asked.

Faye flipped on a flashlight so I could see her face. She wore lipstick and she had a blue towel slung over her shoulder.

"What's up with me is also up with you," she said. "What century is it?"

"The twenty-first."

"That's more modern than 1950, wouldn't you agree?" she asked.

"Yes, Faye."

What is she talking about? I thought.

"A modern woman does not wait for a man to kiss her," she said.

Before I could say a word, Mystery Lady Faye dropped the flashlight and wrapped both arms around me. Then she kissed me. Not a kid-style peck kiss. She kissed me so long I thought she was gonna chew my lips right off my face.

When she finally stopped, I sucked in two lungs worth of fresh air and stared at her with big wide eyes. I open my mouth to say something, but my brain malfunctioned.

"Good night," she said, standing up and pushing the door aside.

"No, Faye, don't leave!" I shouted. She climbed to the ground, then turned and dropped the towel on my face.

"Clean up," she said. "You've got lipstick all over your face."

The door plopped shut and she was gone.

Chapter 18
My Turn to Be Dad

I woke up in a new world. I didn't have to hide from my dad. Maybe I should be hiding from Mystery Lady Faye, but I knew that wouldn't do any good. She was more like a movie star than ever, and I hoped she'd come back tonight.

Too much to think about!

Hoke. The one normal unchanging thing in my life was Cherokee Johnny and basketball.

"Breakfast is ready, son! How about we eat at the table?" Dad's voice brought me back to the strange happenings of last night. Basketball would have to wait.

When I entered the kitchen, my eyes went to the chair where I was sitting the last time I was in the house. Dad saw.

"Yeah, Bobby," he said. "I've been thinking about it too. That's why I wanted to eat here, to get this over with. You hoke?"

"Yeah, Dad, I'm hoke," I said. "I'm sorry about your cut."

"It's me who should be sorry. But, hey! I'm gonna make it up to you."

The table was already set and the kitchen was filled with the sweet aroma of fried eggs and bacon. Dad stood up to serve the eggs and bacon.

"Let me do it, Dad," I said. "You cooked breakfast. Let me serve it."

"Sounds good to me."

So my father and I had our first breakfast together.

When I reached for my orange juice glass, Dad put his hands over his face. He was remembering the orange juice and blood on the floor.

"Ohhh," he moaned. "I am so ashamed of myself."

"Me, too, Dad. I'm ashamed of things I thought about you."

"You gonna practice today?" he asked as we finished eating.

"Yeah, me and Johnny will shoot some hoops, play a few games if anybody else shows up." Then I remembered I hadn't done any chores in at least a week. "Uh, Dad, is it hoke if I wash your truck first, before basketball?"

Dad just looked at me. I had heard about role reversal, but this was ridiculous! He started laughing, then I joined him. We laughed so hard I thought I'd toss my breakfast all over the table. It was maybe the best laugh of my life.

A few days later I moved back to the house. But several days a week I'd ask Dad if I could spend the night in my underground room. He always said yes. Before leaving for work, Dad always told me the chore for the day.

I knew he'd come home for lunch. That was always his first-beer-of-the-day time. And that didn't change, though he did cut back—from three or four to one or two. After work, Dad got into the habit of driving by the park before coming home. If Johnny and I were playing, he'd honk and wave.

One afternoon, Dad parked his truck and watched us shoot three-pointers for a while. Next thing we knew, he was sitting at the picnic table by the basketball court. Johnny and I just looked at each other. This was a little strange, but still hoke.

"Can I take a shot?" Dad finally asked. He stood up and Johnny tossed him the ball. Dad dribbled it a few times, then arched a long shot from the corner. If I had not seen it myself, I would never have believed it.

The ball swished through the net without touching the rim!

"Hoke, guys," Dad said, laughing. "That was total luck, I promise you. I haven't shot a basketball in twenty years."

"Wow," Johnny and I said at the same time. Dad shrugged his shoulders and returned to the picnic table. Mission accomplished. He was one of us, a real live basketball player.

That night when he turned my light out and said good night, I told him, "Nice shot, Dad."

"A sign from above, Bobby," he said. I fell asleep thinking that one over.

School finally started. I walked Faye to school, met her in the hall between classes, and tried to sneak a kiss at least once a day.

Basketball practice didn't start for six weeks. But every afternoon, Coach Robison left a few basketballs out for us to play pick-up games. Unsupervised. That was state rules. No coaching till October 15.

Back home I noticed a disturbing change in Dad—a return to his old ways. Dad was drinking more. With no one around the house, nothing to do but watch TV and drink, he was slipping. He even yelled at me once.

I was in my room doing math homework. He came in late, around eight o'clock. I knew he'd been to the bar.

"Clean this kitchen up!" he shouted. Then he banged his fist against the door, like he used to do. I ran downstairs as fast as I could.

"Sorry, Dad," I said. "Won't happen again." I pretended not to be afraid.

Dad must have realized what he had done. He disappeared into his room and shut the door.

The next morning I got up an hour early and fixed eggs and bacon for us both. Dad gave me a funny look when he entered the kitchen. I filled his coffee cup and sat down. I was just about to cut my fried egg when Dad held his hand up.

"Let me say a little prayer first," he said. I closed my eyes and bowed my head. Mom was always the one to lead the prayers.

"Dear Lord," he said in a quiet voice, "thank you for this food, thank you for my family, and thank you especially for my son, Bobby."

This was his way of saying he was sorry for yelling at me. When I opened my eyes, his head was still bowed.

"I miss her," he whispered.

"So do I, Dad," I said.

We had not spoken of my mother all summer long.

Chapter 19
Got It Bad, My Man

October 15, the first day of official practice, came sooner than expected.

"Panthers come in all sizes!" Jimmy said, welcoming us to the team.

"Don't you mean all colors?" Darrell said, but he had a big smile on his face. Johnny and I were teammates of the Nahullos now, and they stood up for us in the halls, too. Jimmy and Darrell—the two guys who battled and finally beat us on the playground—were even better than we remembered.

The first week of practice went well. I guess I could shoot a three-point shot better than anybody else on the team. And Johnny was his usual inside self, hard to score against and a great rebounder.

But playing on your high school basketball team is very different from playing at your neighborhood park. When you're playing on a team, you have a coach. Mr. Robison was not a bad coach. As long as you did everything he wanted, he was cool. But throw one bad pass, take one stupid shoot, and "WHIRRRRRRRRR!"

When Coach Robison blew his whistle, everything stopped. Everybody froze. Not like on TV when the refs call a foul and play stops.

No, I mean everything *froze*. No one moved a muscle. We all waited to see how many laps we'd have to run.

"Faster!" Coach Robison yelled while we ran laps around the gym. "Don't get lazy on me!" After a few days of running laps, every muscle in my body was sore. But Dad was cool. He had supper waiting every night when I got home from practice. And the list of chores grew shorter.

And he tried to hide his beer cans so I wouldn't know how drunk he was.

A few days before our first game, just after practice, Coach Robison called everybody together.

"We're gonna be tough to beat, guys. If we play as hard as we can, we'll win some ball games. Now, listen up. Here's our starting lineup." He read from a small notebook he carried with him everywhere.

Of course he knew who the starting lineup was, but somehow reading from his notebook made it more of an honor, more official sounding.

"Starting center, Jimmy Harris. At forward, Johnny Mackey. Small forward, Darrell Blackstone. Point guard, Bart Zimsky. And at shooting guard, Bobby Byington.

We were so cool about it, Johnny and me. We just nodded and low-fived the other starters. But when we climbed into Johnny's car for the trip home, we went crazy!

Johnny turned the volume up as loud as it would go, and I popped in an old Led Zeppelin CD my dad let me borrow.

In the days of my youth
I was told what it means to be
a man.
Now I've reached that age
I've tried to do all those things the
best I can.

"Hey, there's Faye," Johnny shouted. Faye was walking by herself on the sidewalk. "Wanna see if she wants a ride?"

"Naw, man. Let's just give her a hard time."

"It's your funeral," Johnny said. He eased his car to the curb, a few feet from Mystery Lady Faye. She was wearing a dark-blue dress. I walked her to sixth-period class just a few hours ago. She was wearing blue jeans then.

What's up with this? I thought.

"OK, little Bobby," Johnny said, "you're on." He rolled the window down and I was staring at Faye. The cool dude who'd just made starter on the basketball team, where did he go?

"Uh, hey," I mumbled. Johnny hit me in the stomach.

"Hey, chickadee," I said, turning to Faye and bobbing my head up and down.

"Chickadee?" she said, still walking. "That's the best you can do? Stop showing off for your friend, Bobby. Be the nice little boy I know."

"I'll show you nice little boy!" I said, still head bobbing. "Wanna ride home?"

"I'm not going home," Faye said. "In case you didn't notice, I'm dressed for a party."

"Hey, Johnny, stop the car," I said. "This isn't funny. Pull over." Johnny turned off the Zeppelin and we pulled to a halt. I jumped out of the car. Faye folded her arms and looked at me. She didn't smile or smirk. She just looked at me. I felt bad.

"Hoke, I didn't mean to be such a smart aleck," I said. "Hoke, maybe I did. But I'm sorry. Coach Robison just announced the starters on the basketball team, and me and Johnny made the starting five! We were celebrating, that's all."

"I forgive you," Faye said, and she was smiling.

"Now, what's this about a party?"

"I didn't say I was going to a party!" Faye said, and now she was LOLing. "I said I was *dressed* for a party!"

"What's the difference?"

"I already went to the party. It was the first meeting of the year of the Latin Club. We thought we'd have a party, maybe attract new members."

"The Latin Club?"

"Gee, I wish I'd known," Johnny said, leaning his head out the window. "Who needs basketball when you've got *the Latin Club*?"

"I'm going to ignore that because you are Bobby's friend," Faye said, but she had that sweet smile on her face. "When's the first game?"

"Next Friday," I said. "Please come. Please?"

"I wouldn't miss it, Bobby," she said. "And maybe some time in your room after the game?"

"I'll bring the popcorn," I said, and before she could change her mind, I jumped in the car.

"Later!" I yelled as we pulled away. Johnny put the pedal to the metal, as Dad would say, and Led Zeppelin screamed again.

> *No matter how I try*
> *I find my way is still the same old jazz.*
> *Good times, bad times*
> *You know I've had my share.*
> *When my woman left home with a brown-eyed man*
> *I still don't seem to care.*

"Zeppelin never knew Faye," I said.

"What do you mean?" Johnny asked.

"I think they'd miss my Mystery Lady if they knew her. I know if Faye left home, I'd be gone too, trailing after her."

"So if you had to choose between basketball and Faye, you'd choose Faye?"

"I'm just glad I don't have to make that choice," I replied.

I glanced in the rearview mirror. Mystery Lady Faye had not moved. She knew I was watching her. She tilted her head and smoothed her long dark hair over her shoulder. The next thing she did made me jump out of my seat.

"What's up?" Johnny asked.

"Nothing," I whispered. "Uh, Faye just blew me a kiss."

"You've got it bad, my man," Johnny said. "I mean bad."

Chapter 20
Baptism by Car

"You nervous?" Dad asked. We were sitting on the patio two hours before tip-off.

"Yeah. But I'm hoping once the game starts I'll be hoke."

"First-game jitters," Dad said, taking a long sip from his third beer of the afternoon. "Want a ride to the game?"

Before I could answer, Johnny pulled into the driveway and honked.

"No, thanks," I said. "Johnny's giving me a ride."

"Have a good game. Play hard. I'll see you there."

"Thanks, Dad."

Thus began the most frightening night of my life.

The gym was packed. Everybody in town wanted to see if this year's team was a winner. When we starters took the court for the opening tip-off, I scanned the stands for my dad. He wasn't there.

I hated it, but I couldn't help remembering No Name, how his dad was never there for him. We lost the opening tip and the Doaksville guard dribbled down court for what looked like an easy, wide-open lay-up. He even smiled as he took off for the shot.

Didn't happen how he hoped.

Jimmy Harris waited for the ball to leave his hand. He slapped the basketball so hard against the backboard it came sailing to me. I took a dribble and passed the ball to Johnny. He crossed midcourt, and when he tossed the ball to me I heard Coach Robison holler, "Shoot!"

What was I to do? He's the coach. It felt so sweet when it left my hand. *SWISH!* The crowd yelled louder and our cheerleaders jumped up and down.

Panthers, Panthers,
Fight, fight, fight!

I didn't know what to do. I just stood there.

"Get back on defense," Coach hollered, and I came out of my trance.

The whole first half went like that first basket. By halftime, we were up by twenty points. I was exhausted and dripping in sweat, but we were winning!

I was in shape. That wasn't the problem. It was the excitement, the energy, the yelling and cheering after every shot, every rebound, every everything!

Coach Robison gave us a short pep talk at halftime. "They will come back," he said. "Expect it. Play tough defense, don't foul, and only shoot when you are open."

As we took the court for the second half, he yelled, "Remember! Defense and share the basketball!"

I nodded and cast one more look into the stands. Still no Dad.

Then I spotted him, staggering through the front door. He threw money on the ticket table and pounded his fist when they were too slow giving him the ticket.

I didn't want to be playing. I wanted to disappear, to climb into my hole. We lost the tip and my man dribbled by me for a lay-up. He faked Johnny out before shooting, and Johnny fouled him.

A three-point play to start the second half, and it was my fault.

"You okay?" Coach Robison asked as I ran by the bench.

I nodded. But I was not hoke. My dad was being led out of the gym by the local police. Two minutes later Coach Robison benched me. The principal had called him over during a time-out. I didn't have to ask. Coach Robison knew about my dad showing up drunk for my first basketball game.

"You've played a great game, Bobby," he said, patting me on the shoulder. "Take a break. You've earned it."

We won the game by twenty-five points. I scored fifteen, all in the first half. I didn't shower or celebrate after the game. I threw my clothes on and headed to the door. Parents and friends were all waiting to greet us, but I ignored even Faye and ran to the parking lot.

He was waiting for me. I knew he would be. A little late, but Dad was there, sitting in his truck at the far end of the lot. His engine was running and his mufflers were roaring.

"Come here, kid!" he yelled. "Who won? You do any good?"

I stood on the curb looking at him. He blinked his headlights and drove by me.

"You too good for your dad, is that it, kid?"

I didn't know what to say. I wanted my new dad back.

"Hey!" Johnny shouted. "Where'd you go in such a hurry? We're all getting together for pizza. Even Coach is coming."

"Can I borrow your car first?" I asked.

"Yeah, sure," he said, digging in his pocket for the keys. Johnny didn't ask where I was going. He saw my dad's truck pulling out of the parking lot. "Meet us as soon as you can at Big Boy's. I'll get us a giant pepperoni. Sound good?"

"Sounds good," I said. "And thanks, Johnny. You played great tonight."

"So did you. Good luck with your dad."

I jumped in his car and adjusted the seat so my short legs could reach the gas pedal. Dad saw me get in Johnny's car, and it made him mad.

He gunned his motor and the truck roared to life. He sped across the parking lot to the four-lane street in front of the school. Dad was easy to follow. He had a bright row of red taillights across the rear of his truck.

When he saw me tailing him he looked in the rearview mirror and shook his fist at me. "No, Dad," I said. It was hard for me not to cry. "I thought you were proud of me."

Then I got mad.

"What am I supposed to do?" I shouted, banging my fist on the dashboard. "I work my tail off, trying to please you. You say you're proud of me, then you show up drunk at my first game." By now I was sobbing. I could barely see the winding road.

Dad took the turns at full speed, and I did my best to follow him. He soon jerked his steering wheel and turned onto a country road, leading to the lake five miles away.

I knew exactly where he was going. He had a favorite drinking spot under a giant red oak tree. He'd park his truck and sit on the tailgate with a six-pack. "This tree is Choctaw," he always said. "If you listen close, it even speaks Choctaw."

I skidded the tires and took off after him, his red taillights blinking in the dust. I was shaking and sobbing and speeding way too fast. But I had him in my sight and he wasn't getting away from me. Johnny's car bounced up and down on the bumpy old road. I skidded from one side to the other to avoid a fallen tree.

Then I saw the lake. It was more beautiful than I remembered. The moon shone on the dark waters, sparkling yellow. My dad's drinking spot, the red oak tree, lay across a two-lane bridge. I didn't see any taillights.

Dad must be already there, I thought. I sped up again to cross the bridge, when my eyes caught sight of somebody standing by the side of the road. It was my dad. He'd parked his truck by the roadside, waiting for me.

And he wasn't mad!

My new dad had returned. His arms lifted to the sky and he had a smile on his face. *He sobered up,* I thought. "Yes!" I shouted.

I don't know what I was thinking. I reached out my arms to greet him and I let go of the steering wheel. The car smashed through a wire fence and rolled into the lake.

Chapter 21
Is This a Dream?

I loved my Choctaw grandmother so much. Of all the old folks in my family, she was my favorite. When I opened my eyes and saw her, I was so happy. She moved her lips to speak, but I couldn't understand anything she was saying.

She wore her favorite dress, the one she was buried in. It was made of light-blue cotton and it moved with the slightest breeze. My mother said she ought to be buried in something more dignified. But Dad and his brothers and sisters all agreed.

"Mawmaw should be buried in the dress she loved the most."

Grandpaw appeared, smiling and whispering, too. But I didn't understand him either. Then Mr. Crocker showed up, the janitor from our elementary school. He was a nice man, pushing his broom up and down the hallway all day long. He died in a trailer house, all by himself.

Soon they were all there. All of the people I had known and loved who had died. They all showed up to welcome me.

"No," I said. I think I was shaking my head. I tried to let them know. "I am not ready to go." They floated away and I was left in the dark.

I don't know how long I slept. When I woke up, Dad was standing by my bedside.

"What chance does he have, Doctor?" he asked. I could not open my eyes, but I knew it was him. He sounded so sad. I tried to speak, but all I could do was lie there and listen.

"Tell us the truth," my mother said. By the sound of their voices, she was standing next to Dad.

How did she get here? I wondered.

"He swallowed so much water," said the doctor. "We are doing all we can to revive him. That's all I can say for now."

"I am so sorry," Dad said. "I know I was a terrible father, but I tried."

"Whatever you tried, it didn't work," my mother said.

"I can tell you this," Dad said. "If he comes back to us, I will never touch another drink as long as I live. You have my word on that."

I wanted to leap high. I wanted to throw the door from my underground room and touch the sky! I wanted to lift my dad and toss him high, toss them both in the air and juggle them up and down till we all flew away to a place where we could be always happy. Always.

But I could not move a muscle. I struggled and lifted one eyelid. Not all the way, but enough to see where Dad stood. He was right beside me.

"I want him back!" Dad said.

Somehow I did it.

I rolled my hand off the bed and my arm touched his. He looked at me and I knew he saw me, the living me, the real me. Just like No Name's dad, he saw me.

"He's going to live," Dad said. "He's not going anywhere!" He leaned over to hug me.

"Careful," said the doctor. "You'll pull the tubes out!"

Dad hugged me anyway, slowly and carefully. So did Mom. When I saw them hug each other, I closed my eyes and fell asleep.

The next time I woke up, I was surrounded by people, just like before—with one major difference. This time everybody was alive. I opened my eyes and everyone clapped.

Dad, Mom, Coach Robison, the entire basketball team, Johnny and his mom and dad, they were all there. I smiled big and flung my head back on the pillow.

But mine wasn't the only head on the pillow. I caught the sweet aroma of rose perfume. I rolled my head to the left and a soft voice whispered, "Hello."

"Whoooooaaaa!" I yelled so loud and jumped so far across the bed that everybody laughed. But not Mystery Lady Faye, the source of the perfume. She tilted her head to one side. She squinted her eyes and ran her fingertips across her cheeks, moving her hair aside.

I looked at Mom and Dad. I glanced at my coach and the team. They were all smiling and nodding, liking what they saw. This was supposed to be a private moment. *What is she doing?* I thought. *She better not try to kiss me!*

I looked back at Faye. She was standing by the bed with her arms wrapped around herself. Her face was glowing and she was laughing, too.

Finally I saw what was happening.

I hid my face in my pillow and wished this moment could last forever. I was alive. I had seen the other side and returned. I had my new dad and my new mom. I had my friends and I had my new girlfriend, Faye. I knew she wasn't Mystery Lady Faye, not really. She was shy and scared and hiding in her own secret room, just like me.

Soon the doctor appeared at the door. "I hate to spoil the party," he said, "but he needs his rest." One at a time, everyone came to my bedside and told me how happy they were that I was hoke. Dad and Mom waited till everyone else was gone. They both knelt by my bed and hugged me so close, closer than ever.

"I am so proud of you both," Mom said.

"This is the beginning of a new life for us all," Dad whispered, and I knew he spoke the truth.

"Will you come to my next basketball game?" I asked Dad.

"We'll both be there," Mom said. "I'm coming home."

About the Author

Tim Tingle is an Oklahoma Choctaw and an award-winning author and storyteller. Every Labor Day, Tingle performs a Choctaw story before Chief Gregory Pyle's State of the Nation Address, a gathering that attracts over ninety thousand tribal members and friends.

In June 2011, Tingle spoke at the Library of Congress and presented his first performance at the Kennedy Center, in Washington, DC. From 2011 to the present, he has been a featured author and storyteller at Choctaw Days, a celebration at the Smithsonian's National Museum of the American Indian honoring the Oklahoma Choctaws.

Tingle's great-great grandfather, John Carnes, walked the Trail of Tears in 1835.

In 1992, Tim retraced the Trail to Choctaw homelands in Mississippi and began recording stories of tribal elders. His first book, *Walking the Choctaw Road*, was the outcome. His first children's book, *Crossing Bok Chitto*, garnered over twenty state and national awards and was an Editor's Choice in the *New York Times* Book Review. *Danny Blackgoat, Navajo Prisoner*, Tim's first PathFinders novel, was a 2014 American Indian Youth Literature Award Honor Book.

Watch Tim Tingle's performance of the traditional Choctaw story *No Name* at the National Museum of the American Indian: youtube.com/watch?v=vdweJ8_qyZE, or do a web search for "No Name Choctaw Film."